More praise for Art Corriveau and *Housewrights*

"In the most wrenching New England love triangle I've read since *Ethan Frome*, Art Corriveau creates a trio of characters in search of their other halves. Exquisitely drafted, *Housewrights* explores loss and longing, friendship and family, the very nature of physical attraction—and ultimately reminds us that home is always where the heart is."

—Jodi Picoult

"This story of a town, a time and a love triangle borrows its rhythms from those of the seasons; Art Corriveau brings a long-dead way of life—the craftsmen and the farmers, the devoted and the venturesome—vividly back to the page."

—Nicholas Delbanco

HOUSEWRIGHTS

ART CORRIVEAU

PENGUIN BOOKS

Corriveau

PENGUIN BOOKS

Published by the Penguin Group
Penguin Putnam Inc., 375 Hudson Street, New York, New York 10014, U.S.A.
Penguin Books Ltd, 80 Strand, London WC2R 0RL, England
Penguin Books Australia Ltd, 250 Camberwell Road,
Camberwell, Victoria 3124, Australia
Penguin Books Canada Ltd, 10 Alcorn Avenue,
Toronto, Ontario, Canada M4V 3B2
Penguin Books India (P) Ltd, 11 Community Centre, Panchsheel Park,
New Delhi – 110 017, India
Penguin Books (N.Z.) Ltd, Cnr Rosedale and Airborne Roads,
Albany, Auckland, New Zealand
Penguin Books (South Africa) (Pty) Ltd, 24 Sturdee Avenue,
Rosebank, Johannesburg 2196, South Africa

Penguin Books Ltd, Registered Offices:
Harmondsworth, Middlesex, England

First published in Penguin Books 2002

1 3 5 7 9 10 8 6 4 2

Publisher's Note
This is a work of fiction. Names, characters, places, and incidents either are the product
of the author's imagination or are used fictitiously, and any resemblance to actual per-
sons, living or dead, business establishments, events, or locales is entirely coincidental.

Library of Congress Cataloging in Publication Data

Corriveau, Art.
Housewrights / Art Corriveau.
p. cm.
ISBN 0-14-200209-7 (pbk.)
I. Title.

PS3603.O689 H68 2002
813'.6—dc21   2001058316

Printed in the United States of America
Set in Janson
Designed by M. Paul

For Raymond and Eileen Corriveau:

Unorthodox parents, unwavering friends,

undeniable housewrights

THANK YOUS

To the artist colony of Yaddo, for six uninterrupted weeks during which most of this story was drafted; to Lori van Dam, for painstakingly buttoning the boots, unlacing the corsets and raising the hems; to Kiera Coffee and Robin Lippincott, for their support as fellow fiction-writers and friends; and to Jennifer Lyons and Caroline White, for believing in my first novel—and then doing something about it.

Monday's child is fair of face

Tuesday's child is full of grace

Wednesday's child is in the know

Thursday's child has far to go

Friday's child is loving and giving

Saturday's child works hard for its living

And a child that's born on the Sabbath Day

is fair and wise and good and gay

—Anonymous

CONTENTS

HOUSEWRIGHTS

1

✿

FAIR OF FACE

[1 9 0 7]

LILY WILLARD DIDN'T LOOK FOR WAYS of foretelling the future. She was only eight years old. She preferred to concern herself with simpler matters, like when school would let out for the summer, how she might coax her pony Buster into jumping apple crates, and whether she would get her own bedroom in the new house. Staying in the moment (this particular moment: her walk home from school one glorious end-of-May afternoon) was generally less complicated than meddling in the next. But Lily found it hard to ignore the signs, especially when they stared her right in the face, especially when there had been two that very morning, both before breakfast.

The first had been a pair of new kittens—one coal black, the other lily white—from a calico barn cat famous for producing much larger litters of all sorts. Lily had discovered this unlikely family under the milk house while fetching a pitcher of cream for the breakfast table. The second sign: a strange two-tone hum emanating from the old crab apple in the orchard caused, she soon discovered, by two competing swarms of insects. Freshly hatched mosquitoes were storming the few remaining blossoms of the lower branches while angry hornets circled a damaged hive higher up in the boughs.

Lily should have been enjoying her freedom from long divi-

sion for the day. Instead, she found herself speculating on what
such a pair of odd pairings in nature might mean. She hoped, for
example, that the kittens didn't foreshadow more Willard children. There were already quite enough of these—three older
brothers and two younger—though another girl, she had to admit, would make a welcome change. The Willard house was by
everyone's reckoning bursting at the seams. So much so that Lily's
father had decided in a fit of the "Februaries" to build a bigger
one. And as far as the dual swarms of insects went, Lily hoped
they didn't predict any plagues of Biblical proportion. She was de-
pending on the success of this year's harvest. A sudden turn of luck
might lead to cutting corners on the new house.

You and your notions! Lily's mother's voice, chiding her for an
overactive imagination. Too few kittens and one too many swarms
probably didn't mean anything. It was 1907. The twentieth century was upon them, and Nature was giving way to Science every
single day. Vermont's cities, all eight of them, had electricity now.
There was talk of bringing telephones to Caledonia County. Not
a week earlier, Lily had seen her first horseless carriage sputtering
up the main street of Cabot Fields.

Lily's musings were interrupted as soon as she rounded the
next bend in the Peacham Farm Road. For parked in her parents'
yard was the strangest vehicle she had ever seen. It resembled a
hay cart, and must surely have been one at some point. It had
oaken wheels as tall as she, a long wooden flatbed and two enormous old workhorses hitched to its traces. But where the hay
should have been sat a tiny white house complete with clapboard
sides, four-pane windows, green shutters and a crooked tin chimney poking out of a shingle roof—as if the Willard family's new
house in miniature had been delivered to the front door.

Third sign of the day? Things usually came in threes, folks
said. Fulfillment of the morning's two earlier signs? Or just a
wagonload of gypsies? Lily quickened her steps home.

The mystery lasted only as long as it took her to reach the front porch. There she found her father mopping his brow with a red bandanna and sharing a mason jar of his dandelion wine with the tallest man she had ever seen. The stranger had giant hob-nailed boots and tree-trunk legs that tapered up to a narrow chest, spindly arms and a gooselike neck. His head was too small for the rest of his body and a little pointy. He was, Lily thought, shaped like the letter "A". It wasn't until the stranger winked his right eye at her in an attempt to be friendly that she realized his left one was made of glass.

"Here's Lily," her father said, flushed from the late-afternoon sun and the wine. "Lily is both my eldest and youngest daughter. Meet Mr. Pritchard, Lil. He'll be building our new house for us." The tall man tipped the brim of his straw hat and accepted the mason jar from Lily's father.

"I'm getting my own room," Lily said, crawling into her father's lap. She saw no reason to beat around the bush. She had already learned in eight long years to profit from half-empty mason jars while they were still half-full.

Both men laughed and continued their conversation about pine clapboards and ash windowsills, the merits of a slate roof versus cedar shingle. Lily soon tired of this grown-up obsession with detail and slipped away from her father's sweaty grip to have a closer look at a curious, large book resting open on the wicker table between the two men. Plate XIX, The Sheridan. A drawing of a big white house with a porch on three sides and a two-story kitchen ell. On the opposite page were three complicated grids covered over with a wreck of angles and curves and arrows.

"What's this?" Lily asked Mr. Pritchard.

"That's your new home," Mr. Pritchard said. "More or less."

"It's called a floor plan," Lily's father said.

"It's like the boot print a house might leave behind, if it could get up and walk away," Mr. Pritchard explained.

"Like your house," Lily said.

Mr. Pritchard scratched his head. "I don't have a house," he said, then checked himself. "Oh, you mean the wagon." He winked at Lily, understanding her. She decided that she wasn't very afraid of him, then, in spite of his giant size and wandering eye.

"It's what he builds the house from," Lily's father said, not understanding at all. "He can look at these floor plans and frame up the entire place. He reads them like maps. Do you understand?"

Lily nodded. She also knew not to trust everything men said when they were drinking. She took the book and reinstalled herself on the porch steps to investigate it more thoroughly. "Though mind you, Pritchard," her father continued over her shoulder, "we'll need to do something about that kitchen. Given where the barn is, the ell should really be on the west side, not the east." Lily gathered up the unruly auburn curls that had, as usual, escaped from her ribbon and tucked them behind her ears.

The book was called *Payne's Encyclopedia of Rural Residences*, by Clarence Payne. (Lily could already read well above her grade level, to her teacher's dismay.) It was full of drawings of pretty houses accompanied by these so-called floor plans. She quickly flipped through the book. Her father hadn't chosen badly at all. The Sheridan was a fine house, much nicer than The Dorset, The Oxford or The Somerset. Not quite as elegant as either The Wellington or The Kent; but these last two were absolutely enormous and Lily wasn't by nature a greedy girl.

The diagram of her new house blurring. Curves and angles rearranging themselves into a completely different floor plan— one that feels truer than The Sheridan. Lines in motion again, cascading like pitched hay, bifurcating, dividing into two separate houses. Two houses now, huddled under the same roof.

Lily rubbed her eyes. Pollen? The orchard was just past

blooming. She returned the pattern book to the table between the
two men. *Stay in the moment.* She decided not to have a glass of
milk in the kitchen. Her mother would be waiting for her there.
She wasn't ready to buckle down to her afternoon chores. Instead,
she crossed the yard for a closer look at Mr. Pritchard's wagon-
house. Bolted to either clapboard side, though obscured by coils
of rope, ladders and various long-handled tools, were identical
weather-worn signs:

ABEL PRITCHARD, HOUSEWRIGHT

CARPENTRY, EBENISTRY, REPAIR

REFERENCES UPON REQUEST

Lily wondered how she might peek into one of the windows. She
was still in her school clothes—a calico pinafore sprinkled all over
with forget-me-nots—which would make climbing up the side a
little tricky. She circled the wagon until she was out of her father's
line of sight. She considered taking off her good boots, to avoid an
inevitable scuff or two, but she decided she didn't have the patience for all the buttons. So she grabbed the rungs of a hanging
ladder and hiked herself up onto the spokes of the rear wheel. As
she progressed up the hub and rim, she thought about the swarm
of hornets in the orchard that morning. She should salvage the
abandoned hive for her new bedroom before her brothers got to
it first. After supper, this would require a long stick for poking it
off its branch from the safety of a lower limb. Lily was a veteran
tree climber, having trailed after three older brothers for most of
her life. She maneuvered herself onto the ladder hanging just below the cabin's window. Her plan was to shimmy sideways along
its rungs until she could see in. But these operations were interrupted by the muffled sounds of movement inside. Did Mr.
Pritchard have a dog? Suddenly the curtains parted above her and

someone threw the window sash up. Out peeked two freckled faces. Lily lost her grip. She fell backward. She heard the soft thud of her body hitting the dirt drive. A puff of dust, two fearful faces staring out the window, blue sky, shooting stars, and then nothing.

The whinny of a horse. The desperate struggle to hang on, the horrifying realization that she won't. The long fall. Screams. Knowing she isn't alone. Not knowing where she is—a dark cupboard? hidden under a quilt?—someplace small but, because of the darkness, infinite—nowhere and everywhere all at once. Sensing that someone is nearby, a loved one trying to bring her back.

Lily woke to blue sky and the sound of starlings warring in the maples above. The same two freckled faces were staring down, now much closer than before. Boys her own age, skinny, tow-headed boys with brown, almond-shaped eyes. Twins.

"You fainted," one of them said.

"For how long?" she asked.

"Not very long," said the other. "We didn't even have time to slap you across the face or pour water on your head."

"You weren't going to get a grown-up?"

The two boys exchanged glances. "We didn't think of that," the first one admitted. "You want us to fetch our father?"

"I think I'm okay," Lily said, sitting up. More little white stars. The tick of insects in the long grass.

"Why didn't you just knock?" the first one said.

"I didn't think of that," Lily said.

The twins invited her into the wagon for a cool glass of water. She accepted gladly; she still wanted to see the inside. The first boy helped her to her feet, which she thought kind though unnecessary. She felt fine, apart from a bump forming on the back of her head. They led her around the back, to a little wooden door hanging off the rear axle. This they had left open in their haste to see if Lily was dead. Just inside were five miniature stairs leading up into the flatbed. Lily climbed them slowly, marveling at the incredible clutter around her. It was just a room, really; but every available inch of wall was covered like the outside with carpentry tools, some of which Lily recognized—hammers, hand saws, wood chisels —some of which were a mystery. Jumbled in among the tools and hanging from the ceiling were skillets, pots and pans, a tea kettle, an egg beater, a fiddle. One of the twins told her to take a seat at the trestle table in the far end while the other dipped a ladleful of water into a glass from a galvanized milk can.

Lily soon discovered, as she sipped her water, that the kind boy's name was Oren. He was the elder twin by thirteen minutes. The other one was Ian. The twins had lost their mother the day they were born. It was probably Ian's fault because his umbilical cord had gotten tangled up somehow in her innards, she learned, but their father had never really blamed him because life was just like that sometimes. The twins had been raised by their father. They had always lived in this caravan, as far as they knew. They were both planning to become carpenters themselves as soon as they were old enough. Theirs was a fine life, they thought; they saw little reason to change it.

"But where do all of you sleep?" Lily asked.

Ian explained that the table folded down to become their father's bed at night. During the day, the benches stored his bedding, his pillow and a good change of clothes. Oren reached up to the long cupboard above their heads and pulled the two handles. It opened down to reveal a bunk filled with stacked blankets and pillows. This was where he and his brother slept, he explained. There was even a little roof hatch that they could open whenever they wanted to see the stars at night or let out the woodsmoke from the pokey pot-bellied stove.

Lily wasn't sure whether she felt pity for these boys who had never had a real home, or jealousy. "We've got new kittens," she said. "Two of them, born just this morning. Do you want to see?"

"You have green eyes like a cat," Oren said.

"And red hair like a pony," Ian added, "only curlier."

"We're Irish," Lily said. "Do you want to see the kittens or not?"

They both nodded. They weren't allowed to have pets, Oren told her. But what about their two Belgians? Lily asked. The boys shrugged. They had given up trying to ride them, Oren said. The workhorses were so stupid they barely even knew they were hitched to the wagon. Lily told the twins she would show them how to ride her pony—it was easy—if they were going to be in town long enough. The boys glanced at each other again. They seemed to do this often, as though they were speaking with their eyes rather than with words. Oren cleared his throat. But they would be living here now, he said, at her farm, at least until their father had finished building her new house. How long would that be? Lily asked. Long enough to learn how to ride, Ian assured her.

While Lily was at supper, Mr. Pritchard parked his portable house near the barn and set his Belgians out to pasture. Lily's father had invited him to supper with the family. But Mr. Pritchard had politely declined. They would be tired enough of him before the summer was out, he had laughed. Best to make good fences from the start. Lily stepped out onto the front porch after the dishes were done and saw that the Pritchards had removed all the ladders and ropes and tools hanging from the wagon and stacked them against the barn. They had attached a tent of striped canvas and mosquito netting to the side from which Lily had fallen. They were now having their own supper in this outdoor room. All three were seated in folding chairs around a folding table, eating, not talking. Roast chicken, she guessed from the smoke wafting out of a clever portable grill. She went back inside. Maybe she could cajole one of her younger brothers into playing checkers.

But that's the way things are when you're a little girl, One day there's nothing but white daisies and a few chickens in your barnyard, the next there's a wagonload of carpenters. Anything seems plausible when you're eight: that your barn cat could only pop out two kittens, that your mother could only pop out boys; that your father would hire a man to build your family another farmhouse next to the one you already lived in; that this man would be shaped like the letter "A" and wear a glass eye and have twin sons about your age. You never question the propriety of anything.

When school finally let out for the summer, Lily did not chase around behind her brothers hoping, as in years past, to be included in their slingshot target practice, games of cowboys-and-Indians or adventures in the back woodlot. House building had by then become an obsession with her. As soon as her morning chores were done, she installed herself under the old crab apple with *Payne's Encyclopedia of Rural Residences* in her lap and, from the tree's cidery shade, monitored the Pritchards' progress against Plate XIX. Unfortunately, it was at the maddening pace of grown-ups.

Mr. Pritchard was still bricking the house's central chimney in alternating rows. Measuring, remeasuring, staking out lengths of twine, choosing bricks from a brown pyramid of them stacked at the site, putting a few back, laying a few, spotting them with his good eye, shifting the twine, measuring again. The chimney was to be an elaborate affair with hearths on all four sides for each of the downstairs and upstairs rooms. Mr. Pritchard needed to work carefully, according to her father, for the flues to draw well. Meanwhile, the boys were digging the root cellar for the kitchen. This they did in complete silence with miniature spades their father must have forged for them. Occasionally, they would add a fieldstone or two to a mountain of them the hired hands had collected throughout spring planting for the new foundation. If the twins communicated at all, it was in that odd language they had of slight nods and fluttering hand gestures. They never spoke to Lily or even acknowledged she was there. All of their initial friendliness had vanished after she had shown them the kittens and let them pet Buster. In Lily's opinion, they were altogether too serious for nine-year-old boys.

One particularly hot morning, Lily made a pitcher of lemonade. She stuffed four jelly glasses in the various pockets of her apron, as well as half a dozen sugar cookies, and brought them out to the Pritchards.

"Now there's a treat!" Mr. Pritchard said, draining two glasses in a row. "Boys, what do you say to Miss Lily, here?"

The twins accepted a full glass and a cookie each and mumbled their thanks. Mr. Pritchard mopped his brow with a very dirty red hanky and drifted over to the chimney. The boys handed back their empty glasses and stared at Lily.

"I dare you to say something else," Lily said. "Anything."

They both glanced at their father. One of them nudged the other, the other cleared his throat. "You promised," he said.

"Promised what?"

"You promised to let us ride your horse."

"Buster's not a horse," Lily said, feeling a twinge of guilt— she had completely forgotten. "He's a pony."

"Well, you promised."

"Oh, all right," Lily said. "For Pete's sake. You can ride him tonight. I'll come and get you after supper."

Satisfied, the one who had done the nudging turned and took up his little spade. The other, the talker—the kind one— stood as if frozen to the spot. She realized she couldn't remember their names.

"Look, I'm sorry," Lily said. "I forgot, what with school and homework and all."

"School," he said, softly. "That's why."

For the first time, it occurred to Lily that the twins probably didn't go to school. They had worked alongside their father all spring while she had suffered with her classmates through the times tables. Mr. Pritchard must teach them at night, by lamplight in the outdoor room, Lily thought. That would be why the lamp burned so late into the evening. "Which one are you again?" she asked.

"Oren," he said. "I'm Oren. You're Lily."

When she came by the tent after supper, both boys were sitting at the table carving little figurines out of wood scraps while their father played the fiddle. Lily was mesmerized. It was marvelous music, lively yet somehow sad at the same time. She sat absolutely still until Mr. Pritchard stopped to rest his fingers. She clapped and he bowed. She told him that one day she would like to learn how to play herself—though it had not occurred to her until that very moment. He flushed and his real eye sparkled. She was welcome to come by and listen anytime, he told her.

She asked the boys what they were making. Mr. Pritchard told her they were carving chess pieces. She asked him if it was a bad time to take the twins riding. Mr. Pritchard eyed the two of them suspiciously. Lily quickly added that it had been her father's suggestion, provided, of course, that it was all right with him. Mr. Pritchard said he didn't see the harm, as long as the boys were back by dark. He warned them not to make nuisances of themselves.

Lily led them into the barn. She showed them how to saddle Buster. She asked them why they were carving chess pieces. One of the boys told her their father sold chess sets on the side. Did they play chess? Lily asked. Maybe they could teach her how. She loved checkers. No, the other said. None of them knew how to play. Their father had shown them which pieces to carve out of a library book. Anyway, it was good practice for all the other things they had to carve, the first one said. What sort of things? Lily asked. Banisters and door frames, he said. Coffins.

"I can never tell the two of you apart," Lily said, changing the subject.

"I'm Oren," the one standing nearest to her said. But it was the other one, Ian, who offered to stroke Buster's nose while Lily harnessed him up. Oren stood by, just out of reach, watching. Buster wasn't going to be good with him. Horses could smell fear. They took advantage whenever possible. Buster would try to throw Oren, sure as anything.

"How does your father tell you apart?" Lily asked.

"He can't," Oren said.

"He doesn't have to," Ian added. "We're always together."

Lily couldn't imagine such a thing, but she didn't say so. She led them out to the back pasture. It wasn't good manners to pry into other people's lives—at least not directly. According to her mother, you found out what you needed to know from sewing circles and horseshoe matches and Sunday school. There were also the signs, of course: which trees were swarmed with insects, what colors a litter of kittens were born, whose babies were born with cauls on their faces. But Lily now kept her interpretation of these to herself. You needed a professional seer to read the signs, according to her mother, like Mme. LeTourneau on the Molly Brook Road. Everything else was just "notions."

Buster did throw Oren. He insisted on going first because he was the oldest. He was showing off, Lily knew. The pony began trotting the moment Oren settled onto his back. Lily shouted to rein him in, but Oren didn't know what that meant; he began whipping the reins against the side of Buster's neck. This was all Buster needed to break into a full gallop. It looked as though he might charge right through the barbed-wire fence. What do we do? Ian yelped. Lily shrugged. This was one of Buster's oldest tricks; he had done the same with her three elder brothers. Buster would stop a couple of yards from the fence and pitch poor Oren over it. Lily and Ian watched this come to pass. Then they both raced across the pasture to Oren's rescue. They slowed to a walk, though, when they saw Oren's face peer up above the wheat grass and milkweed. He was grinning.

To Oren's credit, he insisted on riding Buster back to the barn. All of Lily's brothers had refused to mount Buster ever again, threatening instead to poison his oats. By then, the pony had resigned himself to behaving, as long as he was allowed to walk a few paces ahead of everyone. Ian wasn't the slightest bit afraid of Buster, even after Oren's spill. And Buster took to him immediately, nuzzling and teasing him for carrots. Ian was able to ride around the paddock without incident, managing to get a canter out of him, something even Lily was hard-pressed to do. Ian's eyes were shining when he finally dismounted. Both boys were happy to help Lily comb the pony down, muck out his stall and lay in a fresh bed of hay.

"So what is the difference between a pony and a horse?" Oren asked.

"Ponies are just baby horses," Ian said.

"Not really," Lily said. "Buster is full-grown. Baby horses are called colts. Ponies are a type of horse, bred to be smaller. Buster's what you call a Shetland. I've got a book on them if you want to borrow it."

Another glance between the boys.

"Never mind," Oren said.

"It's all right," Lily said. "I've got your father's book on house building."

"We can't read," Oren said. "Our father hasn't gotten around to teaching us yet."

Lily tried to hide how surprised she was by this piece of news. Surely it couldn't be legal to keep the boys out of school? Everybody went to school. She would ask her father about this later, when she went to give him a good-night kiss. "Well then," Lily said. "I guess I'll have to teach you how to do *that*, too." They all laughed. Lily knew she wouldn't tell her father about the boys. It was clear, somehow, that their illiteracy would be a secret among them.

The next day, Lily crocheted two yarn bracelets while she sat vigil under the crab apple: a black one for Oren because he had adopted the black kitten and named it Rook, a white one for Ian after his white kitten, Knight. Well, not really adopted; more like borrowed. Mr. Pritchard was adamant about them not growing attached to things they would have to leave behind. Lily insisted they wear their bracelets from that day forward. Maybe their father didn't care which was which, but she did.

She spent the rest of her summer teaching them how to read and ride. Which sort of lesson they got was weather-dependent. They would ride on hot afternoons, once the twins had stopped work for the day; they would read when it rained. Lily had the twins mostly to herself. Her brothers had taken little interest in them. The Pritchards were the help, according to her eldest brother. Besides that, they were quiet like girls and didn't know how to play any games.

Lily started them on *Little Men*, skipping the babyish primers she had been forced to endure. It was slow going for most of the cellar-digging and chimney-building—the weather had been unusually dry—but once they began laying the fieldstone foundation, the twins could stumble through a paragraph or two at a time. Neither was very excited about this. But they loved riding Buster and knew that, as far as Lily was concerned, it was a package price.

When it came to riding, the twins were much more enthusiastic pupils. Both could saddle Buster up, both could coax a canter out of him, both could put him into a lather. Buster grew to accept Oren—remarkable, in some ways, because the pony was known for holding very long grudges—but he clearly favored Ian, whinnying whenever he approached the corral. Buster still refused to jump apple crates, however, for any of them. This suited Lily just fine. Animals that minded every command had no spirit, her father always said.

Mr. Pritchard began framing the walls after second mowing. Because this was men's work, he got permission from Lily's father to draft one of the field hands into his service. Together, they dug a sawpit, laying timbers across the top and cutting them to the right length with a two-man saw. Once properly sized, these were laid out on the ground around the foundation, one wall at a time. Lily continued her morning vigil beneath the crab apple and, in the process, learned a fair amount about post-and-beam construction: that the wedges Mr. Pritchard notched into the top of the vertical posts were called tenons; that the recesses he bored out of the connecting horizontal beam were called mortises; that all the tenons must eventually be fitted into the mortises like great petals of an elaborate wooden lotus; that the framed-up sides were then pinned together with long wooden dowels called trunnels; that this was accomplished by boring holes through adjoining timbers with a cross-handled auger and tapping the trunnels into these holes with an oaken maul. The most the Pritchard twins could do throughout this painstaking process was fetch water for the two men and rake up woodchips to be carved into bishops and pawns and queens. By lunchtime, they usually found themselves seated beneath the crab apple with Lily, swatting flies.

The raising of the house's first wall happened on the first of August. The three children had loitered at the site most of the morning while the hired hands hoisted the north face onto the fieldstone foundation with long-handled pikes. But watching the crew affix the angled corner braces between supporting posts became too tedious for such a stifling day.

"Books or Buster?" Lily asked.

"Too hot," Oren moaned.

"Can't we do something different?" Ian asked.

Lily thought about this. Poor boys. All they ever did was work. There were loads of things they could do, of course. The Willards had more than five hundred acres. At breakfast, Lily's mother packed her brothers each a sandwich. After chores, they set off across the pasture in a loud baying pack and didn't return until just before evening milking. They must be doing *something* fun during all that time.

"Come on," Lily said.

"Where?" Ian said.

"You'll see."

She wasn't exactly sure where she was taking them. But once they were in the woodlot, she got her bearings. Someplace cool. She just hoped her brothers weren't already there. She didn't know what she feared more: that her brothers would never like Oren and Ian, or that they would, once they got to know the twins better, steal them away from her.

"This path is an old Indian trail," she said. "Our farm is actually on Indian hunting grounds." This latter part was true; most Vermont farmland had belonged to the Indians at one time. Her first statement might also be true, though the path they were on could just as easily have been made by long-dead cows.

"What kind of Indians?" Oren asked, glancing at his brother.

"What do you mean what kind?" Lily said. "You know, *Indians.*"

"I mean which tribe?"

"Who cares which tribe?" Lily said. In fact, she had no idea which tribes of Indians had inhabited the area. She just sensed them around her. She was going to get caught in one of her flights of fancy again—one of her notions—which irritated her.

"We're part Indian," Oren said. "Abenaki."

Lily stopped and turned. "Really?" They didn't look a bit Indian—who ever heard of blond Indians? But, she had to admit, they did have funny almond-shaped eyes.

Oren nodded.

"Don't expect us to know how to shoot a bow-and-arrow or anything," Ian said. "We've never met any of our Indian kin. We're not even supposed to tell anyone about it." He punched Oren hard in the arm.

"Why not?"

"Our father doesn't want us to," Oren said. "It's bad for business."

"Is that why you don't have a house—because your caravan is like a modern-day teepee?"

"No," Ian said. "We don't have a house because we don't want one."

Lily considered this. "Well if I were part Indian, I would try and make it rain about now. It's so damn hot."

The boys laughed, scandalized by her cursing. She breathed a secret sigh of relief. She had not offended them. This gave her the confidence to lead them deeper into the woods. Luck was with her; her brothers weren't at the swimming hole. It was one of the prettiest places Lily knew: a minor branch of the Waits River that wound its way through the pines until it tumbled over several huge boulders and cascaded into a pool deep enough for swimming. Oren asked if it was her family's. Lily shrugged. She had never really thought about it before. It might be on her father's land, but that wasn't how it really worked. Half the town knew about the swimming hole. No one ever got kicked out for trespassing.

Oren went to the water's edge and dipped his fingers in.

Warm, he reported. Ian strolled over and crouched next to him. Lily felt a pang of jealousy. She had always wanted a sister. She couldn't imagine what it would be like to have someone right there beside you, sharing what you were feeling, understanding when you said things like it was warm.

"There's a rope," Lily said, to remind them she was there. "In that swamp willow. You can swing out from the rock below it and dive into the deepest part. Can either of you swim?" She regretted asking this immediately. She was always making it sound as though they couldn't do anything. She didn't think that. They could dig a root cellar. They could lay a fieldstone foundation. They could carve fancy little chess pieccs. They just didn't seem able to do anything normal.

Ian stood and unbuttoned his shirt. Oren, grinning, followed suit. Soon they were both naked and diving in. Lily wasn't quite sure what to do. "Are you coming or not?" Ian called from the center of the pool. "It's like heaven."

"I didn't bring a bathing suit," Lily said, kicking at an imaginary tuft of something.

"Neither did we."

She began unbuttoning her boots. It was completely inappropriate to be swimming naked with these two boys. She knew this from her mother's endless litanies on what little girls did and did not do. They did not climb trees, they did not jump ponies; they did play with dolls, they did bake cookies. But it was so damn hot. And nobody was around. And she couldn't think what harm it would do. So she unlaced her apron and unbuttoned her frock, dropped her hose and her underwear to the ground. With a whoop, she cannonballed into the pool.

They swam together. They had contests to see who could dive out farthest from the rope swing. They found a stand of choke cherry bushes and painted warrior stripes all over their faces and bodies. They made a ring of smooth stones and built a pretend fire out of sumac stalks, then danced around it, whooping to bring on the rain. They dove back into the pool to wash their war paint away. She told them the three "su" words that were pronounced "sh"—sumac, sugar and sure. She taught them her favorite nursery rhyme, the one her father sang whenever they were swinging on the porch together:

> Monday's child is fair of face
> Tuesday's child is full of grace
> Wednesday's child is in the know
> Thursday's child has far to go

Later, the three of them lay drying on a flat rock beneath the swing, humming the rhyme softly to themselves. Lily was between the boys, close enough to smell the pond water evaporating off their shoulders. A gentle breeze tickled the down on her arms and legs. A squirrel scolded them from somewhere far up in the willow's branches. A yellow butterfly perched on Ian's shoulder, unafraid. Lily closed her eyes. She could tell from the way the sun dappled her lids that it was nearly time to head back to the farm. But she drifted away to a big white house with many gleaming white rooms, all her own, all with big beds made up in different patchwork quilts, a different one for every night. A shadow crossing her face eventually brought her back to the swimming hole. And when she opened her eyes, she saw Ian staring intently at her female parts. "Get away," she said thickly, swatting at him as though he were some giant horsefly.

"I've never seen one of these before," he said. "Look Oren."

Lily closed her legs and sat up.

"No, don't," Ian said. "Let my brother see, too. We'll let you look at ours."

"I don't need to look at yours," Lily said. "I've got five brothers. I know what it looks like."

"Please?" Oren said.

Lily sighed dramatically and opened her legs. Oren sat up and joined his brother's inspection of her privates. He was shier than Ian, but just as curious. And in spite of Lily's scorn, she had a good look at their things, too. Identical, like the rest of them. This gave her an idea. If she searched hard enough, she might find a mark somewhere, a mole or blemish that distinguished them naturally. They each submitted patiently to a full inspection. Nothing. Nothing that Lily could find, anyway.

All three realized at the same time how late it was. They dressed quickly and ran back through the woods to the farm. Out in the open fields, Lily saw that it was very late indeed—well past supper. They would all catch hell.

Catch hell they did, but not for being late. Lily's brothers had been playing in the woods after all. They had followed her and the twins to spy on them. They had watched them swim and dance naked around the fire ring. They had run home and tattled to Lily's mother. Luckily, they had not stayed long enough to witness the examination—another secret the three of them now shared. Lily was sent to bed without the plate her mother had kept warm. From her window, she could hear the twins being whipped in the caravan. And she could see that three sides of the Willards' new house had been raised while they were off playing in the woods.

It all changed after that. Lily's father banished her from the building site and forbade her from spending her afternoons with the Pritchard boys. She was in serious trouble, she knew, when her father meted out the punishment. She could usually rely upon him to intercede with her mother. Lily's mother did not deliver her customary lecture on the appropriate behavior of little girls. Instead, she burst disconcertingly into tears. She apologized for not providing Lily with any sisters. The two of them would do more things together, she promised, once the morning chores were over: sew a patchwork quilt, bake cookies, dry summer flowers in the family Bible.

Lily decided to behave like a proper little girl for the rest of the summer—or at least until her parents forgot about the swimming hole incident. She wanted her own room too much to risk the company of the twins. Meantime, she needed to take matters into her own hands. She loved her mother, she really did. And she admired her. But her mother never laughed or joked. And the thought of spending the entire day with her, sewing and baking, threw Lily into a panic.

At Sunday school, Lily befriended Hallie Burke, the prissiest girl in the class. She feigned interest in paper dolls and pinafores until Hallie invited her over to play. Lily's mother was overjoyed. The Burkes were well-to-do. Hallie was always at the center of a gaggle of girls. Lily trudged into town every afternoon with grim determination.

Behaving like a proper little girl was harder than it looked. Hallie liked to host elaborate tea parties for her dolls. She had a miniature set of china cups and saucers for these events, which she claimed was imported from Boston. She encouraged Lily to bring along a few of her most favorite dolls. Lily usually grabbed whichever ones were at the top of her toy chest. Hallie was outraged by the state of their dresses. Then again, she was equally as critical of Lily's appearance. You'd almost be a pretty girl, Hallie would say, pouring out imaginary tea, if only you would tame that red mop of yours and stay out of the sun. How did she ever expect to attract a prince that way? Lily would fidget distractedly. Grown-ups spent all of their free time talking and worrying about What If. She couldn't imagine how a little girl could prefer this to riding a horse or swimming. She was quite happy to marry a farmer, Lily would say, just like her father. Hallie would offer a plate of invisible sandwiches and counsel her to set sights higher, on a minister, or a banker at the very least.

Lily's brothers finally took an interest in the Pritchards. They began teaching the twins how to play baseball, which they apparently liked. Otherwise, it was cowboys-and-Indians. From what Lily could tell, her brothers always made the Pritchards be the Indians. She wondered if Oren and Ian had foolishly told them about their ancestry. She never got close enough to ask. She watched them from the road on her way to and from Hallie's. Occasionally, Oren would stop whatever he was doing to wave. She was too lonely and jealous to wave back. Instead, she would gaze off in the direction of the building site. The house was really taking shape now; it had walls and floors, staircases and a roof. She was reassured to see, even in skeletal form, that it looked just like The Sheridan in *Payne's Encyclopedia of Rural Residences.*

One morning, Hallie's mother sent word that Hallie had come down with a fever and couldn't come over to bake cookies. Lily read quietly in her room, thankful for the break. At lunch, her father announced he would be making an inspection of the new house. She asked if she could tag along—it just came out. She had nothing else to do, she added, while Hallie was laid up. Her father eyed her suspiciously and then broke into a grin. Sure, he said, why not.

He was in fine spirits as they wandered from room to imaginary room, climbing ladders and crossing catwalk planking. The Pritchards were making excellent progress. When they stopped at the north corner of the second floor, her father asked if she could guess where they were. She put her hand in his and squeezed it. Apparently, he had forgiven her.

It was climbing around in the scaffolding of the new house that gave her the idea of a treehouse. Later that afternoon, she was pretending to read on the front porch. Mr. Pritchard had lent her two more house-building books: *The Country Builder's Assistant* and *The American Builder's Companion* by Asher Benjamin. Both were full of beautiful but incomprehensible diagrams for carving columns and fireplaces, door frames and staircases, all with classic Greek proportions and patterns. Slowly, she flipped through pages without really looking at them while she eavesdropped on the boys. They too had stationed themselves on the porch after lunch to decide how they would spend their afternoon. Her brothers thought it too hot to play a running game like baseball; the twins fretted that their father would put them to work stacking odd ends of lumber if he saw them idling about. The old crab apple popped into Lily's head—and hornets circling an empty hive. She had never bothered to retrieve it for her room. She wondered if it was still there.

"I know what to do," she said.

"Nobody asked you," her eldest brother snarled.

"Yeah, why don't you get lost," the middle one said. In her mind, she never named her brothers. She rarely bothered with names at all—of cousins or classmates, teachers or townsfolk—if the people attached to them were likely to remain outside the small soap bubble of a world she liked to blow for herself and then inhabit.

She looked over at Oren and Ian. The three of them hadn't really spoken since the swimming hole.

"Wait," Oren said. "She usually has good ideas."

"No, she doesn't. She's a girl," her eldest brother said.

"What is it, Lily?" Oren continued, ignoring him.

Lily bit her tongue and waited.

"Well, what?" her brother said, crossly.

"A treehouse. We can build one with the scrap lumber. I know the perfect tree."

"Who's we?" her brother said. "You and the turd in your

pocket?" Her other two brothers guffawed. The twins didn't join in. Soon her brothers stopped. "She can't help us make it," the eldest said. "She doesn't know how."

"What have you ever built?" Lily asked.

Her brother glowered at her.

"It doesn't matter," Oren said. "It's Lily's idea."

"Well, I'm not building any stupid treehouse if she's helping," the eldest said. The others murmured their assent.

"Suit yourselves," Oren said. "Come on, Lily. Let's go take a look at your tree."

She could have kissed him.

Of course her brothers followed along. Their disparaging remarks and catcalls quickly gave way to enthusiasm when the twins began to discuss a treehouse with two floors connected by a ladder. They had their own set of tools—everything, really, they needed to get the thing built—two hand saws, two hammers, a folding yardstick, a square, a bubble level, a chalk line. Soon they were all busy lugging scrap lumber from the building site to the crab apple. Lily was made to fetch a large sheet of butcher's paper from the pantry, along with a pencil. Her mother, who was darning at the kitchen table, asked what she was up to. Making a get-well card for Hallie, she fibbed.

Back in the orchard, Oren drew out the plans for the treehouse while Ian directed the other boys in setting up a rope hoist to get four-by-sixes to the appropriate limbs. Oren's drawing was beautiful. And by now Lily was familiar enough with *Payne's Encyclopedia* to read it. There would be windows with shutters that could be closed against the rain, a trap door entrance, and a lookout platform on the roof. Lily suggested a swing. Oren happily added one to his design.

"Are you sure we have enough wood for all this?" Lily asked.

"No," Oren said, grinning. "But I don't know how to build any of it, anyway."

Lily smiled back. "I missed you," she said. It just sort of popped out. She couldn't even remember thinking it.

"We missed you, too," Oren said. "Now I'd better help Ian with that hoist before your brothers drop a beam on his head."

They got the first platform built by milking time, when Lily's brothers had to leave off hammering and sawing and get to the barn. Lily lingered behind. She had not been alone with the twins since the swimming hole. She didn't know when she would have the opportunity again. She sat with Oren at the platform's edge, dangling her feet with his. Together they watched Ian take out his pocketknife and begin carving into the tree's trunk. What are you doing? Lily asked. Making our mark, Ian said. Oren explained that somewhere, in every house or barn or church they built, they carved a secret symbol that named the place: a dove or skull-and-crossbones, a pineapple or double-bladed ax. They never told anyone about these symbols—not even their father. They were housewrights. They always moved on, they rarely ever returned. They were never allowed to share meals or have pets or make friends. But they always tried to leave a little piece of themselves behind, always took a little piece away with them.

It's an angel, Lily whispered.

Ian laughed. No, he teased. It's a bumble bee. He joined them at the platform's edge when he finished. Together, they sat and watched the sun disappear behind the woodlot. Lily noticed their bracelets were getting frayed. Oren's black one had faded, and Ian's white one was so soiled that they were approaching the same shade of gray. She would have to make new ones before long, she said. Oren smiled and told her it probably wouldn't be necessary. When Lily asked him why, both boys stood, turned away from her and dropped their trousers. Oren's buttocks were criss-crossed with red welts. Ian's buttocks were smooth, but his upper thighs were similarly scarred.

"Now you'll always be able to tell us apart," Oren giggled.

Lily tried to laugh along with them. But in truth, she didn't find this new secret all that funny.

The treehouse was like so many good ideas: a lot easier to start than finish. It was harvest time at the Willard farm, and Lily's brothers were called into the fields to hay. There was corn to chop and crib, soldier beans to pick and sift, potatoes to dig and sack. Lily was confined to the kitchen most days, helping to make preserves from the red and black raspberry bushes her mother kept, as well as from wild choke cherries, blueberries and windfall crab apples. Out of an endless supply of cucumbers, Lily and her mother made dill, bread-and-butter, sour crock, gherkin, sweet-tongue and Christmas pickles. They made piccalilli out of green tomatoes and canned the red ones. They canned green beans, wax beans, beets, carrots and new potatoes—and whatever else there was.

Once the clapboarding and windows went up in the new house, the Pritchards moved inside with their tools to build the kitchen cupboards, make pantry shelves, finish off the staircases and carve the wainscoting. Lily saw very little of them. Suddenly it was autumn. Time to go back to long division and multiplication tables, to calico dresses and woolen hose.

One night at supper, Lily's father announced that their new house was finally finished. They would be moving in on Saturday. Lily and her brothers boxed up their books and toys on Friday night before going to bed. They made sure their clothes were all neatly folded in their dresser drawers. They rearranged the hangers in their wardrobes so that they were all facing in the same direction. Lily didn't sleep well that night. It felt too much like Christmas. Her dreams about a long night of waiting were mixed with the night noises around her. She woke once to see a woman staring out her bedroom window, her body flickering and glowing with a strange halo of orange light. Then she really woke. She saw that her two younger brothers were asleep in the next bed. After that she gave up on sleep altogether. She dressed and sat in the kitchen rocker until her father came down at first light.

The neighboring menfolk arrived for breakfast. Lily and her mother made ham and eggs, baked beans, stacks of buttermilk pancakes with maple syrup, black coffee. They all ate standing on the porch, quiet, anticipating the morning ahead. First the menfolk moved the cook stove. Then the ice box, then the hutch where her mother kept the good china. After that, bedsteads and mattresses, dressers without their drawers. Lily's job was to keep pitchers of ice tea and lemonade full, and to wander among the workers with fresh glasses.

The womenfolk showed up at noon with their children, bearing cold plates of sliced roast beef and turkey, fresh baked bread, last year's pickles and canned fruit, potato and bean salads, every imaginable sort of pie. After a picnic lunch, the children were sent off to the swimming hole. The women then took up dresser drawers, quilts and blankets, armloads of clothes on hangers, and ferried them over to the new house, gossiping like magpies along the way.

It wasn't until after lunch that Lily remembered about the Pritchards. She went out to the caravan to invite the twins to swim. They were breaking down the outside room. The table and sink and grill had vanished. The ladders and coils of rope and tools had been stowed in their proper places on the sides of the wagon.

"Where are you going?" Lily asked in a panic. "There's plenty to eat. And they'll have horseshoes and music later. You can fiddle, Mr. Pritchard."

"I expect you'll get along just fine without us," Mr. Pritchard said, winking. "You like your new room?"

"Very much," Lily said. "But please stay for the party. You've worked so hard and done such a good job. It looks just like The Sheridan."

"Got to be moving on," Mr. Pritchard said.

"Where?"

"Your father has written to one of your relations on the Derby Line. They got a barn that needs a new addition before the snow flies. I guess you better make your good-byes to the boys now."

Lily walked with them down to the treehouse. "Maybe you'll be back next summer, so you can finish it," she said.

"Doubt it," Ian said. "We're never in the same place twice. Can I take a quick turn on Buster?"

Lily nodded, trying to hold the tears back. She and Oren watched him go. "I never got to teach you how to write," Lily snuffled.

"I'll be back," Oren said after a moment.

"Good," Lily said, "I'm sure your father would get work just about anywhere around these parts."

"No," Oren said, taking her hand. "For you, I mean."

"Oh," Lily said. "You mean someday."

"I think you're the most beautiful girl in the world."

"You're only nine years old, what do you know about it?" Lily said.

"Ten," Oren said. "We had a birthday." He reached over and kissed her on the lips. Salty, dry. Lily didn't put much store by it, but it seemed to make Oren happy. He insisted on holding hands all the way back to the barn. When was their birthday?

Walking hand in hand. Losing track of where they are walking, and when. Leaves blowing all around them, wind biting into their wool. The smell of moss and damp stone—root cellar smells. He is taller, taller and stronger. But just as remote, a shadow. Will he ever be stronger than she? A grackle screeching overhead. The smell of cut hay, summoning her back.

Oren, like his brother, took a final ride around the paddock. The twins said good-bye to Rook and Knight, their kittens. By then Mr. Pritchard had unblocked the wheels of the caravan and moved it down to the drive. He was shaking her mother's hand, accepting a fat envelope and a slap on the back from her father. Lily walked the boys over and watched them climb into the cab of the wagon. She held her father's hand as the Pritchards drove off down the Peacham Farm Road, swirling dust behind them.

That afternoon the menfolk removed all the windows and doors from the old house and fitted them into the remaining gaps of the new. Then there was roast pig and horseshoes, fiddle music and dancing. There was also a surprise, something completely un-expected. At sunset, the men moved the scrap pile of wood up onto the porch of the old house and poured a five-gallon can of kerosene over it. Lily's father set the old house aflame with a torch. The dancing and music carried on by the light of the blaze. It didn't take long for the old house to burn to the ground. Then it was time for everyone to go home: the neighbors to their beds, the Willards to their old beds in their new home. But as Lily climbed the stairs to her very own room she had a funny feeling in her stomach, that she would never feel like she was going home—not really—ever again.

2

Full of Grace

[1917 - 1918]

Lily loved her job as town librarian—to be surrounded each and every day by books!—but the summers were long. About all she had to look forward to was the post, the odd book salesman, lunch at Hallie Burke's house, and late-blooming tigerlilies along the Peacham Farm Road on her walk home. Her only visitors from June to September were doddering old men who came in to escape the heat of the little attic rooms their sons gave them. These old-timers would install themselves at a shiny oak table by the window, prop huge tomes of Civil War battles in front of them, debate the current war raging in Europe for a moment, and then doze off. Enveloped in a slow swirl of silence and dust motes, Lily's only recourse was to dredge up more efficient ways of organizing the reference books. Not a single child came in. Without school history projects and homework assignments, the need to know what made the wind blow or which presidents were assassinated, the children forgot about her completely.

She missed them keenly. She missed their boundless energy, their harmless pranks, their unabashed affection for her. In their absence, she longed to be a child again herself: dirty-faced and wild-haired, sneaking wads of her father's chewing tobacco, running barefoot in the back woodlot, jumping Buster. Without children around, she found it hard to sustain her disguise as a proper young lady. On a lovely summer's afternoon, her pleated skirt and ruffled waist risked tumbling to the ground. Given half a chance, a headstrong tomboy named Lily would happily dive naked into a wooded swimming hole when no one was looking.

Well, the children would be returning from their fathers' hay fields to keep her company soon enough. Lily had noticed on her walk to work that the maples of Mount Mansfield were slowly changing from green to gold and russet. Soon the apples of the Willard orchard would follow suit, the morning dew would turn to frost, and the flavor of mown hay in the air would give over to woodsmoke.

Lily glanced at the wall clock and sighed. She wrote out three notices for overdue books, addressed and stamped the envelopes, and set them on the edge of her desk for the postman. She sighed again. May as well dust from A to L. She armed herself with the feather duster and went for the fiction shelves. She hummed quietly as she removed books, dusted their titles and returned them to their proper places. One of the old-timers glared at her. She stopped humming.

Still, she supposed, it was better than ending up a farmer's wife. Nothing but back-breaking labor from sunrise to sunset, your hands stained red by berries or bleached white by lye soap, kept eternally pregnant as the cows you milked twice a day, no contact with anyone beyond the front gate except Sundays when you got the chance to nod to other farm wives at church. Lily's poor mother. A woman who at forty-six looked sixty. A woman with absolutely nothing to say at supper, who left conversation entirely up to her husband, her daughter and the two sons she had living at home. Lily's mother listened to the talk, though—with more hunger than for her own meals. But she had long ago given up on trying to make her day of cooking, cleaning and canning sound interesting to anyone, including herself.

Already at Dickens. How would she make this last?

Hanging by her fingernails from the highest shelf. Slipping. No grit, nothing to grip onto—she keeps a tidy library—every oaken shelf gleaming with lemon-scented beeswax. Falling. A row of books tumbling with her: Dickens, Emerson, Flaubert, Goethe. Lying broken on the polished wood floors, buried under a cascade of leather-bound volumes. Eternity passing. No one to hear her scream.

Lily tucked *Oliver Twist* into place and set her feather duster aside. Still daydreaming, still unmooring herself from the here and now, like she did when she was a little girl. *You and your notions.* At least she no longer believed everything she dreamed up now. The welcome squeal of the library's swollen door. Patrons to attend to, thank goodness. She didn't recognize the young man who stood peering around, adjusting his eyes to the light. He was big and handsome, not from Cabot Fields. He had taken off his hat, as though he were at church. This he clutched in front of him. Scarred, callused hands.

"Can I help you?" Lily asked.

"I'm looking for the librarian," he said, clearing his throat.

"You've found her," Lily said. "Anything else?"

The young man broke into a grin. "I was expecting somebody older," he said. "My letters aren't so good. Sometimes I tell the librarian what I'd like to say and she helps me put it down."

"Of course," Lily said. "Come have a seat at my table."

Lily pulled out a pad of stationery from the top drawer of her desk. Librarians wrote a surprising amount of correspondence for people—mostly official letters requesting information or registering complaint. Though nearly everyone in Cabot Fields knew how to read and write, they were not always confident about expressing themselves formally. Lily dated the top of a clean sheet. "Return address?" she prompted.

"Skip that part," the man said.

"Addressee?" Lily murmured.

"The person I'm writing to, you mean?"

Lily colored slightly. She was being too officious; it was one of her faults, borne of competence and boredom. This poor young man was probably finding it hard enough to ask for help. "Yes, that's right, that's what I meant," she said apologetically.

"I'm writing to Lily Willard."

Lily's pen froze. She looked up. She did not recognize him, she didn't know him. He was not one of the parade of traveling book salesmen who turned up at the library once a year. They generally wore threadbare suits and were literate, if not altogether polite. So why on earth was this young man writing to her?

"She lives in town here," he said. "Do you know her?"

"I'm Lily Willard," she said.

An uncomfortable moment of silence, the old-timers all staring with unabashed interest. "Lily," he said. "I can't believe it. You're so pretty."

"I'm terribly sorry," Lily said. "But I can't for the life of me—"

"It's Oren," he whispered. He held up his left wrist. Where a watch should have been was a black bracelet, braided of black leather.

Oh, she had thought of the Pritchard twins from time to time growing up. She had wondered in odd moments what had become of them. But they had vanished the day her new house was finished. And because she had never expected to see them again, she had put them out of her mind. Her life had reverted to baking cookies with Hallie, wishing school would get out for the summer, coaxing Buster in vain to jump over apple crates. White bracelet or black? Was Oren the boy who had been good with animals, or the one who had kissed her good-bye? Gone was the towheaded freckle-face in either case. In his place stood a gigantic man with broad shoulders and muscular arms. Big as his father, only much more handsome: golden hair flopping over a strong brow, long thin nose, chiseled jaw, even white teeth. His eyes were the same, though; brown and oddly almond-shaped, fringed in long lashes, like a girl's.

"Goodness me," Lily said. "Oren Pritchard. We'd better have a cup of tea."

Lily learned that Oren was carpentering on his own, now. His father had died a few years earlier. Mr. Pritchard had cut his leg mishandling one of those new, gasoline-powered saws. Progress for you, he had muttered, plastering himself with a compress of cider vinegar and goldenseal. He had refused to see a doctor, of course, and the leg had eventually gone gangrenous. The twins had buried him next to their mother, in a cemetery near Bennington. Not knowing what else to do, Oren and Ian had carried on with the family business, living out of the back of the caravan as they always had, taking the next commission on recommendation from the last. In May, there had been a letter from the U.S. government waiting for Ian in Barre. (For official correspondence, the twins used the post offices in Brattleboro, Barre or Burlington as their forwarding address—all towns at crossroads, all places they passed through at least twice a year.) Ian had been drafted into the army to fight the Germans. He would muster at Fort Ethan Allen in Burlington, be trained by the Vermont National Guard and shipped off to France as part of the 26th Yankee Division. Oren had not been drafted, though he had also registered— either that or his own draft letter had never caught up with him. Oren hadn't heard from Ian since. To make matters worse, the carpentry referrals had all but dried up since the war. People were making do with what they had. Recalling that Lily's father had been very good to them, Oren had decided to write to her about work in the area.

Suddenly it was time to close for the day. Lily invited Oren home to supper. His caravan was parked across the street from the library, beneath the shady maples of the town common. Progress has been made in the intervening years since Lily had last seen the Pritchards. The little portable house no longer sat on a hay cart. It had been moved to the flatbed of an REO truck. Oren proudly showed it off. The REO had a shiny black cab and four enormous rubber tires. Oren helped Lily into the cab. Wooden steering wheel, leather seats, road map of Vermont, a ring-stained teacup.

With a great chugging and huffing and grinding of gears, they headed down Main Street. Lily hoped that no one could see her. She knew, though, that everyone would hear about her ride home. The old-timers at the library were vicious gossips. To hide her embarrassment, she began to talk. She told Oren about her father's decision to switch from Holsteins to Jerseys. They were more prone to illness but their milk sold better because it was fatter. She told him about the death of her second eldest brother. His horse had reared at the backfire of a Model T. He'd been thrown beneath the horse's hooves and his skull had been crushed. She told him about her eldest brother's plans to start a maple syruping operation. He was putting up a sugarhouse down by the farm's largest maple grove. Maybe Oren could help him build it.

Oren turned his truck off the Peacham Farm Road and braked it for a moment at the foot of the drive. He stared up at the house. "The Sheridan," he said.

"It's always made a lovely home," Lily said, "even though there are fewer of us now."

"We did good work on this one," Oren said. "We liked it here."

Lily's brother did hire Oren to build a sugarhouse that September. Then her father had him repair the milk house. After that, Hallie Burke's husband hired him to convert their summer kitchen into an indoor toilet. Lily didn't see much of Oren. She got busy with the schoolchildren and knitting socks for the war effort, saving peach pits for gas masks. In fact, she forgot all about him until the day he began working at Hallie's.

She turned up, as usual, for lunch and noticed that Hallie had set the table for three. Hallie told her the extra plate was for Oren. But he's not expecting it, Lily whispered; he's the help, not company. You weren't supposed to break bread with them. Boundaries were important. Hallie laughed at the very idea and called Oren to the table. Lily was right, of course. Oren balked when he saw the extra place setting. He had his own food out in the caravan, he said. Nonsense, Hallie said, there was plenty— ham salad stretched to infinity. She told him to wash his hands and take a seat. He did as he was told. But as soon as he had wolfed a sandwich, he excused himself. The strong silent type, Hallie said. She hadn't noticed him fidgeting throughout the meal. She was an inveterate chatterbox who rarely looked for repartee. It was a quality in social situations that Lily, who wasn't much of a conversationalist, admired. Most other times, though, she shut out Hallie's endless prattle, wondering how Hallie's husband could stand such a steady diet of it.

Hallie invited Oren for pea soup the next day and, to Lily's surprise, he joined them. The day after that it was baked beans and Oren turned up at the kitchen table without even being called, his hands already washed. Lily began to look forward to Oren's presence at lunch. He never said much—it was hard to get a word in edgewise with Hallie—but when he did venture an observation, it was surprisingly witty. Hallie flirted outrageously, rarely catching on to the fact that she was often the brunt of his gentle jokes; she thought he was flirting back. Lily knew, though, that Oren's wry jabs were meant for her entertainment, not Hallie's. They were a way of sharing something private, something special. He never talked about his own life, never once brought up the fact that he had a twin who was somewhere off in Europe fighting the Germans. A secret they shared. Lily felt ridiculously flattered by this. She decided that Oren would never be the type of person to host a party. He was the type you would always invite as social glue. He added *something*, even if you weren't quite sure what.

By Indian Summer, the new water closet was ready. Hallie made a special lunch of ham and potatoes. Lily brought the last of the season's mums for the table. She could tell that Oren was touched by their little going-away party. Hallie gave him a wristwatch. The town jeweler had recently begun carrying them, now that army officers in France had made them popular with men back home. She insisted he try it on, then and there. She noticed his frayed leather bracelet and threatened to take a scissors to it. How would he ever find more work—or a wife—wearing such an awful thing? Oren strapped the watch over the bracelet without comment.

Later, when the two women were doing dishes, Hallie admitted that she felt guilty about Oren—about not being able to put him onto more work. "Times are hard," she said. "As it is, I've had him repair every hinge and creaky floorboard in the place. I've run out of things for him to carpenter."

"You've been more than fair," Lily said.

"Oh it's not just that," Hallie sighed. "I've gotten used to having him around. It doesn't look like children are in the cards for me. And I get lonely, wandering around this huge house by myself all day."

"You'll still have me," Lily offered.

"Well you're not six-foot-six and as broad in the shoulders as a barn door."

Oren was sweeping up the last of the sawdust in the new water closet when Lily went to say good-bye. She saw immediately that he had taken the watch off. He wouldn't wear it every day, she knew. What use did he have for time? He would save something like a wristwatch for best. She doubted somehow that he encountered many watch-wearing occasions. When he saw her, he set the broom aside.

"I didn't get you a gift," she said.

"I know what I'd like."

"What's that?"

"For you to show me someplace special."

"I don't understand."

"You did that once before," he said. "Remember? You showed me and Ian that swimming hole. I'll never forget it."

Lily flushed. That's not all she had showed them, if memory served. It was the first time Oren had brought Ian up since their meeting in the library. "All right," she said. "When?"

"How about right now?"

"But the library," she said.

"Close it. Just this one afternoon. For me."

"All right," she said.

They walked together to the library. He waited on the front steps while she made a sign that read the library was closed for reasons beyond her control. Then she led him up the Peacham Farm Road in the opposite direction of the Willard place. They walked in silence. The sun was bright and the king maples lining the road were in full autumn fire. Oren reached for Lily's hand. She let him take it.

If there were four perfect days a year—one for each season—one would be the first real snowstorm; another would be when the lilacs burst into bloom; a third the golden light after the last haying; and the fourth the turning of the maples at their peak.

Eventually, they reached a rusty iron gate a couple of miles outside of town. "It's Cabot Fields' first graveyard," Lily said, pulling the gate open and stepping through. She led him into what appeared to be a stand of paper birches and pointed to what was left of the tombstones, broken like bad teeth. "Practically no one remembers that it's here, except for a few of the old-timers at the library." She crouched to clear yellow leaves away from one of the slate slabs. They could barely make out any names or dates, so scrubbed away by time were the inscriptions. Lily explained to Oren how the original town of Cabot Fields had been located just beyond the rise of the hill. There was nothing left of it now, she told him, except a crumbling chimney or two among the pines. The Indians kept burning the town to the ground. After three or four fires, the founding fathers finally smartened up and asked the local chief why his tribe was so hostile about the English settling in the area. Turned out they weren't. They just couldn't have the white men building their longhouses on sacred ground. And sure enough, once the settlers moved Cabot Fields to the valley, the Indians never bothered them again.

"What kind of Indians?" Oren asked.

"Abenaki," Lily said. "Your people."

"You remembered."

"I did some reading up on the subject. I'm a librarian."

Oren sat in the leaves, using the tombstone they had uncovered as a backrest. He patted the ground between his legs. Lily hesitated for a moment, then sat. She rested her own back against his chest. She let him wrap his huge arms around her. (He *was* broader than a barn door.) Together, they contemplated the sky through a latticework of branches. She closed her eyes and listened, listened to the creak of the birch branches above, listened to the rustle of leaves dancing in the rising wind, listened to the thump of Oren's heart.

"Would you ever marry me, Lily?" he whispered into her ear.

"Shh," she said. "Listen, listen carefully."

They both listened. And sure enough, they heard a faint metallic tinkle, off to their left. "What's that?" Oren asked.

"It's a tin bell. In the old days they were strung alongside every gravestone."

"What for?"

"For rescue," Lily said. "In case you weren't really dead. Imagine if you happened to wake out of a deathlike sleep to discover you were six feet under? They made coffins back then with tiny panes of glass in the lids, positioned at eye-level. They placed a ring around your little finger, one that was attached to a wire so you could ring a little bell on your tombstone."

"How often did people need rescue?"

Lily waited for another gust of wind, another jangle of the bell. She led him to one of the slate markers poking up out of the leaves and loam. They found the bell next to it, tangled in a stand of ferns. It was dull gray and made of crude tin. It dangled rustily from an iron rod stuck into the ground. A thin wire ran from the rod, along the edge of the stone, and into the ground. Lily had never seen one herself; she had only heard about them from the old-timers. Most had already been gathered up by enterprising locals and sold off as antiques.

"Take it," Lily said. "It's worth money."

"You haven't answered my question, Lily," Oren said.

"A while back, some local families mounted a campaign to move the town fathers buried in this cemetery to the new one," Lily said. "But according to the old-timers, they abandoned the project as soon as they began unearthing coffins where the rotted satin linings had been torn to shreds by fingers long since turned to bones."

"That's not the question I meant," Oren said.

"I don't want to bump around the back roads of Vermont in a truck the rest of my life. I like it here. And I like my job."

"I like it here, too."

"You'd settle down?"

"I could make chairs and tables, or linen chests when anyone wanted one. People always need a place to sit."

"Chess sets," Lily said. "People always need them, too."

"Don't tease me, Lily. Answer my question."

"How do you feel about raising a few horses?"

"Is that a yes?"

"I guess you'd better kiss me," Lily said.

It was nicer than the first time. Gentle and moist, hungry. But maybe that was just because she was grown-up now, and knew what kisses were for. They lay in the leaves beside each other, kissing and listening to the lone bell jangling in the wind. They knew without saying so that they would cover it back over and leave it exactly where it was.

That night, Lily took Oren home to supper a second time, to tell her parents the news. Lily's mother was overjoyed; Lily wouldn't be the last girl her age to get married. Fear that her only daughter would end up the lonely spinster of Cabot Fields had been etching a line of worry into her mother's brow. Lily's father, on the other hand, was more skeptical. He had always adored Lily's company and didn't see any problem with her living at home for the rest of her life. She had her own room. What was the rush? I love her, Oren said. He was sitting across the table from Lily's father, sopping up the rest of his gravy with a biscuit. I've always loved her and I always will. That's not going to change whether I wait a week or a year or ten years.

It was downright inappropriate—a man didn't share such intimate thoughts at a Vermont farmer's dinner table—but Lily forgave him. Oren had never had any sort of proper upbringing; he didn't know better. Lily's father stared hard at him, then at her. He took her hand and squeezed it. His was trembling slightly, which touched her. Wait a year, he said to Oren. Make something of yourself here in town. Show me you're not going to drag my daughter off to Christ-knows-where. If you can do that, you'll have my blessing. Meantime, you can park your truck on Lily's land. May as well start thinking about the house you're going to build for her.

And so it was settled. They all had pie. Lily walked Oren out to his truck in the front yard. They kissed. Lily went to bed.

Lily's land was across the Peacham Farm Road from her father's. It was only thirty acres and not well suited to farming—the soil was stony because a brook ran though it. (Lily's father had always assumed she would marry a local boy and end up farming his place, anyway.) But it had a knoll at its center that was fairly clear of the hemlocks that plagued most of the acreage. It was really the only suitable spot for a house. Lily took Oren up to see it the next day at lunch time. She had Oren park his truck at the foot of the hill, where the haying track ended. From here it would still be possible to get to the road once the snow flew. She pointed out the brook—the water was clean enough to drink—and then led him up to the crest for a look around.

"This is yours?" he whispered.

She saw her surroundings through Oren's eyes, then. And it was like waking from a dream and seeing her home for the first time. Rolling green hills all around, rolling back and back like waves until they deepened in hue to indigo, lightening again at the horizon to violet, then sky. She felt like Samuel de Champlain, the first European ever to set eyes on this lush, almost tropical landscape. He had stood at just such a promontory four hundred years earlier and proclaimed what he saw *les Monts-verts*, the Green Mountains. Champlain's Abenaki guides had remained silent. They had been roaming Vermont for a thousand years. This was *Wabenaki* to them, The Dawnland, where the sun slept each night. Its highest peak, Mount Mansfield, was where Tabaldak the Great Spirit lived. You could tell when he took up residence there in the autumn. His great mantle of maples turned from cool greens and blues to fiery crimsons, oranges and yellows. Lily never realized that you could see half of Caledonia County from her little knoll, not to mention Joe's and Molly's Ponds and the spires of St. Johnsbury. Nestled in the valley below was all of Cabot Fields: the white steeple of its First Congregational Church, the white bandstand of its common, the red covered bridge crossing Molly Brook. Two rows of neat white clapboard houses, all with green shutters. A pretty little place, really. A place that didn't like to call undue attention to itself.

"Well, it's ours, now, I guess," Lily said. "My brothers all got a lot more land, though. I expect I'll get the good china. My youngest brother gets the big house. But he and his wife—if he ever stops tom-catting long enough to find one—have got to live in it with my parents and take care of them until they die. And I don't expect that will be for a good long while yet."

Oren chuckled. He rarely laughed out loud, she noticed, though he always had a ready smile. "I meant it, you know," he said, hooking his arm around her waist.

"Meant what?"

"What I said, about always loving you."

"You didn't even recognize me when you waltzed into the library."

"What about you?"

"I didn't recognize you either."

"Will you ever give me a straight answer, I wonder?"

Lily put her hand to Oren's lips. "You've got to give me some time to get used to all this, okay?"

Oren nodded. He reached into his trouser pocket. He took Lily's hand and slipped a simple gold band onto her finger. "My mother's," Oren said, his voice husky. "It's the only thing I have of hers."

Lily flushed with pleasure. "Are you sure?" she whispered.

"We'll build the house here," he said. "Facing southwest."

She understood that he didn't want to discuss what he had just given her. It was too important. "Whatever you say," she said, kissing him on the check. "You're the housewright."

They ate the sandwiches she had packed. They lay in the grass for a few moments, kissing again, staring up at the clouds. Oren was hard under his jeans; she could feel it pressing against her leg. Sex was something she hadn't really thought much about. She would have to ask Hallie about the particulars at some point. She would also have to tell Hallie about her engagement before it got around town. But she needed a few days, she decided, to get used to the idea herself. She kissed Oren once again and left him there to set up camp.

Back at the library, she made a sign for the community bulletin board at the post office:

HANDMADE FURNITURE

TABLES, CHAIRS, CHESTS

YOUR CHOICE OF WOOD

CARPENTRY, CABINET WORK & REPAIRS

ENQUIRE WITH LILY AT THE LIBRARY

Then she sat at her desk and brooded, hidden behind a stack of recently returned books on mathematics, horse husbandry, quilting, Protestant religions and trout fishing. *I'm getting married.* She stared at her hands, willing them to match library cards to backs of books. A simple gold band glinting in the lamplight. She couldn't quite imagine what it would be like, her wedding. She could see herself married to Oren, all right: living up there on the hill, gardening, raising children, making supper. But she couldn't picture the actual event. She just didn't go in for all that prissy stuff about choosing dresses and flowers, ceremonies and cakes. And she didn't have any older sisters to ask for advice. She wondered if there was a book she could read on the subject, tucked away in the Ws.

A few afternoons later, Hallie burst through the library doors, demanding to know what was going on. Lily hadn't been over for lunch in days. Hallie had finally seen her sign at the post office. Had Oren decided to settle in Cabot Fields after all? Lily ushered Hallie into the back room for a cup of tea. She tried to explain about their engagement while the kettle boiled.

Hallie was dismayed. "How could you let me carry on like that, when there was already an understanding between the two of you? I'll never be able to face Oren again."

"But there wasn't any arrangement," Lily said. "It happened so quickly. And not until after he finished up at your house."

"Well *something* must have been going on behind my back."

"I swear. One minute we were talking about Indians, the next he proposed."

"Do you love him?"

"I guess so, or I wouldn't have said yes. I haven't actually had time to think."

Hallie scrutinized Lily's face for signs of deception. A moment passed. Suddenly the anger lines in her face disappeared. She began fussing with the tea bags that the General Store had just started carrying. Lily looked on helplessly as Hallie pulled the kettle off the stove and poured two steaming cups. "Well, have you set a date?" she asked, wringing both teabags out with a spoon.

"Sometime next October."

"Good," Hallie said. "So there's plenty of time to work all that out."

"What do you mean?"

"The love part. Meanwhile, you've got a ton of decisions to make."

"About what?"

Hallie stared at her in disbelief. "We're talking about the most important day of your life, Lily! Big or small? Afternoon or evening?"

"Oh, that. What do you think? I meant to see if there was a book on the subject, but then I got busy."

"That's it!" Hallie cried. "I'm taking over. I'm officially appointing myself as your matron of honor. Don't worry, I'll take care of everything. All you have to do is show up."

Lily wondered whether she should breathe a sigh of relief or begin worrying in earnest. "I suppose I should think about making a dress," Lily ventured.

"Nonsense, you'll wear mine. We just need to raise the hem and take out a few of the ruffles—the simpler the better with a war on. But we will have to tat you a completely new veil. Mine got torn on a floorboard at the church. I think a morning ceremony, don't you? Followed by a breakfast. Everybody's doing breakfasts these days. Besides, you've got to feed the relatives coming in from out of town. And I doubt that Oren has much family in the area."

Hallie prattled on happily. Lily let her, keeping an eye peeled for any patrons in the front room. By closing time, Hallie had decided the actual date in October (the last Saturday), the time of day (late morning), the reception location (Lily's mother's house), the food (steak and eggs, followed by cake and ice cream), and the guest list (virtually everyone in town). Lily's mother would need to throw an engagement party over the summer, preferably in July. Lily wondered on her walk home to the farm how she would break this alarming bit of news to her. Odd, really. Even with all the details of her wedding decided, Lily still could

not close her eyes and picture herself standing at the church altar
in Hallie's dress. In fact, she could not remember a single detail
about Hallie's wedding though it had taken place little more than
a year before.

Lily's sign at the post office was a great success. Oren was
busy throughout the winter, making Christmas-present chests
and dressers, rocking chairs and rocking horses. With the leftover
scraps of oak and maple he carved chessmen. A few of the sets he
sold to townspeople as gifts. But most of them were bought up by
Lily's traveling booksellers, who took them down-country to re-
tail in Boston and Hartford, wherever they were from.

Oren made time each afternoon to stop by the library. He
would sit at the window table with the old-timers. Some days it
was to read or practice his writing—he told Lily he couldn't have
the town librarian marrying an illiterate man—others it was to
work on the drawings for their house. Lily didn't get to spend
much time with him; the holiday season was busy. But she encouraged him whenever she could by recommending books, correct-
ing his spelling, and peeking over his shoulder as he sketched out
their new life together. Their house would be beautiful—and un-
like anything she had ever seen. It sprouted porches and towers
and windows everywhere. More like a fairy-tale castle than a
house you would actually live in. Lily was reminded of the designs
he had done on brown butchers' paper for their childhood treehouse. With those he had also allowed his imagination free reign.
What had he said when she asked him to add a swing? Something
like: why not? I don't know how to build the rest of it either.

Any of Lily's father's misgivings about the match were soon
laid to rest. Oren was hard-working and talented—everyone said
so. He came to supper every Thursday and Sunday night. He was
much more talkative than he had ever been at Hallie's. He would

often share what he had read at the library that day (he was particularly interested in ancient Greece and Rome) or he would get
Lily's father started on horses—the merits of Morgans over Belgians or the maladies particular to Shetland ponies—and this
would carry them through the meal. Another surprise: the two
men took to playing chess afterward. Oren had learned the rules
somewhere in his travels, and he happily taught her father the basics. Oren always won, which impressed her father, prompting
him to insist on a rematch the next night he was over.

The rest of the time, Oren lived by himself in the caravan. It
never occurred to Lily to visit him there until they celebrated her
nineteenth birthday. He invited her over for supper. Not knowing
what to make of this, she donned her everyday wool coat and
boots and began the snowy trek to the caravan. She wasn't expecting much. Her brothers were absolutely useless in the kitchen,
though they tried every year to make a hunters' breakfast for
their friends at the opening of deer season. What they most often
made was a big mess. But it was the thought, she supposed, that
counted.

She knew she had underestimated Oren's domestic abilities
as soon as she crossed the Peacham Farm Road. Lining the shoveled path to the caravan were lanterns made out of paper sacks,
each with a candle flickering inside. The mouth-watering aroma
of roasted chicken wafted from the outside room, which looked
like a large lantern itself because its roll-down canvas walls were
lit from the inside by candles, dozens of them, candles hanging
from hurricane flues in the bamboo rafters, candles around the
perimeter of the dirt floor, candles stacked in tiers on a table ele-
gantly set for two. She worried for a moment that she would be
cold, having supper outside like that, but she soon realized the
candles were heating the room to a very comfortable temperature.

"Goodness me!" Lily said when Oren emerged from the back of the truck. He had dressed for the occasion (a pang of guilt; she had not) and he had slicked down his hair with some sort of pomade. He really was handsome, she thought, one of the best-looking men she had ever seen.

"Happy birthday," he said, taking her coat and kissing her on the forehead. "Sit, sit. Supper's about ready and I don't want it getting cold."

Roasted chicken with stuffing, mashed potatoes, tinned peas, gravy. It wasn't like anything she might have made—the spicing was very different and there were bits of ham and onion in the peas—but it was good enough to have seconds. There was even a bottle of red wine to go with it. Lily only took a few polite sips, at first. She had never had wine before and doubted she would like it. But once she grew used to its bitter tree-bark taste and how it warmed her stomach, she was surprised to find her glass nearly empty. She let Oren pour her another splash. She still had a bit more chicken on her plate. It was her birthday, after all.

When they finished, Oren told her to close her eyes. He produced a small cake lit by a single candle. Her mother had made it, he confessed; there was really no way to bake in the caravan. It was Lily's favorite, of course: chocolate with chocolate icing. He insisted she make a wish before blowing the candle out. She stared into the flame, trying to conjure something she wanted. But her head was too muddled by the wine and the closeness of the candle-scented air. So in the end she screwed up her eyes and counted to three, then blew.

"Time for your present!" Oren said. His cheeks were flushed and his eyes sparkled. He was being far more playful than usual, and Lily liked it. How much wine had he drunk? The bottle was nearly empty.

"I don't need a present," Lily said. "You're spoiling me, Oren."

"Hush up and close your eyes again."

This she did. He told her to hold out her hands, palms facing up. He placed a light, smooth object in them. She knew instantly what it was: a fiddle. A lovely, shiny fiddle. "But this isn't your father's?" she whispered.

"No," he said, "Ian has that one. But I copied it before he left. It took me more than a few tries to get it right, I'll tell you."

"When did you start making it?"

"Right after you said you wanted to learn."

She had heard Mr. Pritchard play once, ten years ago. She had liked his unusual style of fiddling; she had mentioned in passing that she too would one day like to play. But she had barely given it another thought; she had been eight years old at the time. Oren had obviously thought a great deal more about it. He had spent the intervening years learning how to carve fiddles. Such devotion in a fiancé should have thrilled her. It didn't. It made her anxious. How would she ever live up to it?

"Do you like it? There's a bow coming. I had to order it special from Montpelier and it didn't get here in time."

"It's beautiful. But I never learned how, Oren."

"That's okay. Ian will teach you when he gets back. He plays almost as well as my father did."

"You're mad as a hatter," Lily said. And then she started to cry.

Oren took the fiddle out of her hands and set it on the table. He raised her to her feet and took her in his arms. He let her sob against his chest until her tears ran out. Then he kissed her. She kissed him back. He unbuttoned the front of her dress and shucked her out of its bodice like a fresh ear of corn. He turned her around and unlaced her corset. He turned her back and began kissing her breasts, running his tongue over her nipples, grazing them lightly with his teeth. She sighed. He lifted her into his arms and carried her into the caravan. Mr. Pritchard's bed was made up,

the one that served as a table and benches during the day He laid
her down upon it, then knelt above her, staring into her eyes.
Candles, candles everywhere, all burnt low and guttering. Candles dripping beeswax onto the cabinetry, onto the hanging pots
and pans, onto the cooking utensils and tools around them.
Smoke, wax smoke and the haze of wine.

She drifted back to the swimming hole on that hot summer's
day. The slow flutter of a yellow butterfly's wings. A bronze shoulder to rest upon. Whose? With her finger, she traced the outline
of his excitement. It seemed big, too big. She had five brothers.
She only knew about little boys. I've never seen one of these before, she said thickly. That was a fib. She had seen *this* one before,
just not on a grown man. Oren whispered that he didn't know if
they should. Please? she said, I'll let you see mine. He kissed her
again, hungrier now. She fumbled with the buttons of his trousers
until he helped her.

Later, she looked at him as he lay sleeping on his stomach.
Broad as a barn door. His buttocks were still criss-crossed with
scars, though the angry redness had long since faded away. Scars
from the beating his father had given him for dancing with Ian
and her in the woods—dancing to make the rain come. She wondered about what she had just done. She did not feel guilty. She
would do it again, probably many times, before she got married.
But it had not been the near-sacred experience her mother had
tried, awkwardly, to prepare her for. And she wondered if she
should have waited for her wedding night after all—if that would
have made her feel complete and satisfied, righteous. Less sad.
Still, she liked what they had done together and she hoped, with
practice, they would both get good enough at it to make each
other happy. But tonight, right now, looking at him, she felt oddly
alone. Lonely.

She dressed herself, retrieved her coat and boots. The candles had all gone out; so she made her way by starlight. At the

Peacham Farm Road, she turned back. She had forgotten the fiddle. She went to get it. Oren was breathing heavily in his sleep. She considered crawling back into bed with him, but then decided against it. Tonight, sleep waited for her in her own room.

A thought struck her as she crept up the back stairs. No, it was more like a snippet of conversation that she hadn't completely been able to digest with her meal. Ian will teach you, Oren had said. When he gets back. All this time Lily had been envisioning a future with Oren. Meanwhile, Oren had been envisioning a life—whether he realized it or not—with both her and Ian in it. He hadn't heard from Ian in nearly a year. Yet Ian was in his daily thoughts, was included in his plans for the future. Lily decided she had to know something before she married Oren, something important. Was Ian dead or alive?

Without telling Oren, she began to write letters. She wrote them throughout the new year of 1918 and into the spring. She wrote them on library stationery and left them on the corner of her desk for the postman to take away. She wrote them as though it were the official business of the township of Cabot Fields. She wrote first to Fort Ethan Allen in Burlington. The commander there referred her to the U.S. Army training base outside Paris. From there she was referred to bases farther afield, places in Belgium she had never heard of: Verdun, Messines, Ypres. She would get letters back, letters addressed to her at the library, typed on blue onion skin and bordered in blue and red chevrons. She would have saved the stamps for the children, but there were none. Just inked U.S. Army franks that bled into the blue paper.

Oren began building their house. He started with the root cellar as soon as the ground thawed. He could only work at it a couple of hours a day. He had been maple sugaring with Lily's eldest brother to pay for a load of chimney bricks. Now he was helping out with her father's spring tilling in exchange for any of the better fieldstones they happened to dig up. These they hauled to the knoll with her father's workhorses at the end of each day. He needed a lot of them for the foundation, he claimed. It was going to be a big house.

Twice a week, Lily cooked supper with him at the caravan. The excuse she gave her mother was that they were having a reading or writing lesson. In truth, they made love after they ate. But she always returned to the house to sleep in her own room. She ordered a book on fiddling from the library in Montpelier, and when it came, she began teaching herself how to play. She was determined to learn at least one tune by Oren's birthday in the late summer. It was much harder than it looked. She developed ridges in her fingertips. You had to press down on the strings to get the right notes to come out. She practiced in her room at first—until her father's dogs set to howling. After that, she preferred the privacy of the milk house; its stone walls were thick enough to muffle her squeaks and squawks. She set a couple of rat traps in the tiny storage space in the rafters and hid her fiddle there, along with the music stand she had bought on a trip to Montpelier. One of her father's old three-legged milking stools was the perfect height for it. Lily grew to like being among the whitewashed fieldstones and galvanized milk cans beaded over with condensation. She was so rarely alone, and it was like having a little house of her very own. But she could only take the chill for an hour or so before she lost the feeling in her fingertips.

Lily dreaded her dress fittings at Hallie's. These began to occur in the late spring, about once a fortnight. The two of them would rush through a bowl of soup at lunch. Then Hallie would make Lily stand on an ottoman in her sewing room, encased in a too-tight satin gown while she poked and prodded at her. Lily felt like a giant pin cushion. She would squeeze her eyes shut—to take her mind off the fact that she might topple over in a dead faint—and try to imagine her wedding day. Only distressing images would materialize: of sweat stinging her eyes in a stiflingly hot church; of the suffocating scent of tea roses; of standing in a satin dress so stiff it could just as easily stand there at the altar without her; of scratchy lace cuffs and a long lace veil—lace everywhere—catching on floorboard nails. If Lily kept her eyes open, she had little choice but to stare at herself in Hallie's full-length mirror. In her mind's eye, she had never really grown herself up much. She still saw herself as a grubby little tomboy with cat-green eyes and crazy red hair that cork-screwed out of her scalp. She hardly recognized the slender bride standing there in Hallie's dress. She wasn't bad looking. She might even think, "now there's a pretty young woman," if she saw herself on the street. Curiosity caused her to twist and turn, to get a better look. Hallie would chide her to stop fidgeting then, the words whistling through the pins in her mouth.

But it wasn't just the tedious process of removing ruffles from the bodice and raising the hem that made her uncomfortable. There was also Hallie's stream of questions: what would Lily's mother be wearing, what would her father be wearing? Had Lily ordered the flowers yet from that shop in St. Johnsbury? Should she order extra for the reception in her mother's parlor? What had Lily's mother decided about the cake—white or chocolate? Had Lily asked her mother about the engagement party yet? Lily would usually interrupt Hallie then, explaining that she needed to get back to the library.

"This is going to be so pretty," Hallie would sigh. "It just needs a few more nips and tucks. Think of all the time and money we're saving, Lily."

Lily would bite her lip. She was certain sewing an entirely new dress would have taken her mother half the time. And pattern books from the library's homemaking section were free.

One afternoon in May, the postman delivered a letter to the library, addressed to Lily from a hospital in Boston. Her hands went completely numb as she signed for it. She shoved it into the pocket of her skirt and finished reshelving the returned books. Suddenly she stopped. She went over to the old-timers' table and informed them they would have to leave. What for? they asked. Now, she shouted. Get out! She locked the library as soon as it was empty and began walking down the Peacham Farm Road. She broke into a run. She ran all the way to the knoll where Oren was laying the foundation.

"Here," she gasped, thrusting the letter at him. "Read it."

He set his trowel down and mopped his brow with a hanky. "What is it, Lily?"

"It's about Ian," she said.

Oren took the envelope. He read the return address and glanced up at her. She nodded and tried to smile. He tore the envelope open and unfolded the single sheet of paper it contained. He read it slowly, mouthing out the words, struggling with the ones he didn't know. An eternity seemed to pass. It was all Lily could do to keep from ripping the letter out of his hands. Why hadn't she just opened it in the library? It was addressed to her, after all.

Oren's eyes welled up. "He was shot outside of someplace I can't pronounce. Three bullets in the stomach. They didn't find him till two days after the battle. They took him to Paris. From there they shipped him to Boston."

"Dead or alive?"

"He's alive. It says here that they couldn't identify him for a while. His tags got lost. He doesn't really know who he is."

"Let's go," Lily said, grabbing the letter from his hand.

"To Boston?"

"You'd better get cleaned up. And bring a change of shirt. I'll be over at the house, packing a lunch. Daddy'll lend us his car. Do you have any money?"

"What I saved up to buy the timbers."

"Well, don't just stand there."

They stared at each other for a moment. She flung herself into his arms. They hugged among the stacked fieldstones, crying then laughing. Then Lily took off at a run for the house.

A nurse led them to a sunny room full of bandaged young men in identical dressing gowns. Some were smoking and reading, others were playing cards around a table. Ian was in a wheelchair, off by himself, staring out one of the French doors that opened onto a lovely little garden. The nurse called his name from a few paces away. Ian didn't turn around. She shrugged. Oren squeezed Lily's hand once, and strode over to tap his brother on the shoulder.

Ian looked up. His face bore little resemblance to Oren's now: waxy skin stretched uncomfortably across sharp bones, dark circles obscuring dull, listless eyes. These peered up at Oren with incomprehension at first. But then the thin white line of his mouth crooked into a smile. Ian reached his hand up. Oren bent lower to let Ian stroke his face. A moment passed like this. Oren stooped even lower so that their foreheads touched. He rested his hands on Ian's shoulders and looked deeply into his brother's eyes. Ian raised his hands to Oren's shoulders. They remained like this for several minutes, eyes locked.

Lily fiddled with the hat she had brought but not bothered to pin on. There was that feeling, again. The one she remembered from the swimming hole when she watched the boys testing the water—the one about loss, of never having had a sister.

Finally Oren stood.

"Let's go," he said.

"Go where?" Lily said, nervously.

"Home," he said. "Let's get him home."

3

✿

In the Know

[1 9 1 9]

Lily took to closing the library for two hours every afternoon. No one seemed to notice or care—it was July—except maybe the old-timers who had no place better to go. Everyone else in town was preoccupied with the second mowing, which was late because of a wet June. Lily simply locked the door at noon and didn't open it again until two o'clock, sometimes half past. She didn't bother to make a sign; she didn't have a suitable excuse.

She no longer had lunch with Hallie. The dress was ready. The flowers had been ordered, the reception menu decided upon, the guest list finalized. She felt ridiculously free now, free from the suffocating restraints of planning. She spent her long break at the building site, helping Oren. He was unhappy with his progress, and had taken to fretting about it. By mid-summer, he had only dug the cellar, bricked the chimney and laid the foundation. He was just now cutting timber for the framing. At this rate, the house would not be ready for their wedding. Lily didn't really mind; she was quite happy to sleep in a pile of blankets on the floor, as long as there was a roof over their heads before the snow flew.

Difficult, even, to imagine snow this particular afternoon. Heat so intense that, by Lily's noon walk to the site, it rose up from the Peacham Farm Road in waves, waves that flickered in the glaring light like flames. She felt as though she were swimming in fire: every step forward had the belabored slowness of movement underwater, each gesture creating swirls and eddies of pure heat.

Something swimming toward her, a shark emerging from the shadows of the nearest maple. Mme. LeTourneau, a wispy little French Canadian woman dressed in dark wool, even in this heat. The town seer. You paid Mme. LeTourneau a visit when you lost your mother's wedding ring or if you were worried you weren't going to bear a son. You always brought something with you to her run-down little farmhouse—a side of bacon or a dozen eggs, a gallon of maple syrup—she wouldn't take your money. And you sat at her kitchen table in silence while she took your hand. You waited. It could take her several minutes to speak. And when she did, she would tell you: you would find that ring, but not until years after you had stopped looking for it; you would never have sons, but your daughter would have one, and he would sit at a typewriter all day instead of milking cows—imagine that!—and this particular typewriter would also type pictures as well as words, and everyone would have one of these things eventually, just like everyone had Fords today.

Lily had never paid the old lady a visit.

"Afternoon, Lily," Mme. LeTourneau said.

"My goodness you startled me," Lily said. "I didn't see you there."

"People see what they want to see," Mme. LeTourneau said. "You see more than you let on."

"Beg your pardon?"

"I said, I was probably just stooped over. I'm out looking for goldenseal. You know, my Indian cures."

"Any luck?"

"What's luck got to do with it? I hear you're getting married."

"Later in the fall," Lily said.

"Well, all the best to you," Mme. LeTourneau said. "And give my regards to your mother the next time you're talking with her."

Lily watched Mme. LeTourneau shuffle down the road, her black skirt flapping like the heavy wings of a crow. She shivered. Mme. LeTourneau's farm was at the other end of town, off the Molly Brook Road.

By the time she reached the caravan, she was so drenched in sweat that she had completely forgotten about her encounter with the woman. She stepped out of her dress and hung it from one of the bunk handles, hoping it would dry quickly. She freed herself of her corset, threw it on the bed, and sat for a few blissful moments in her drawers. She poured herself a ladle of water and dribbled it down the back of her neck. She felt instantly better. Reluctantly, she donned a pair of her father's overalls and one of his old cotton shirts. Oren was waiting for her up on the knoll.

She began to fix lunch from whatever was left over in the ice box. Oren kept it remarkably well-stocked with cold roasted meat, leftover boiled potatoes, hard boiled eggs, leaf lettuce, radishes and cucumbers from her mother's kitchen garden. He was a meticulous man; the caravan was as tidy as her mother's kitchen.

Lily thought she heard laughter. She stopped packing a wicker hamper to listen. The chirp of crickets. She smiled: nature laughing. That she was constantly hearing laughter and whispers was a carryover from childhood—her overactive imagination. She couldn't help thinking, though, as she made her daily climb up the knoll, that there wasn't much laughter in her life at the moment. Just plans and more plans. She felt a little anxious when it came to Oren's ambitions. A new house, marriage, winter. It all seemed so far away, vaguely unreal. What felt real to her was the relentless sun on her neck, the hay ticking with crickets, a cloudless, endless sky. Heat.

Ian was up on the summit with Oren.

It was the first time Ian had been out of bed since his injury, as far as she knew. Yet they were working together. Lily watched Oren raise a timber and Ian measure its length, Oren take up a saw while Ian steadied the timber for cutting, Ian position it on a rafter while Oren hammered it into place. Oren was doing all of the real work, but Ian was clearly helping. Lily flushed. She felt as though she were spying. Their work was so intimate, like a moon-lit waltz or whispered conversation between lovers. Oren finally noticed her standing at the edge of the site. He waved her over. Ian smiled and waved too, a beautiful boyish grin that could melt the coldest heart. Was it her imagination, or were they acting slightly sheepish, as if they had just been caught talking about her?

Her imagination. Ian still couldn't speak. His vocal cords had not been damaged, according to Old Doc Perry. "Shell shock" was his opinion on the matter. A newfangled illness—a nervous disorder not a physical one—brought on by modern trench warfare. Doc Perry had done some reading on the subject: utter silence for months on end, screaming in the middle of the night, inability to gut fish or hunt game, inability to eat meat at all. Ian was probably just not yet ready to talk about what he had seen, Doc Perry told Lily and Oren. Give it time. Time was something Ian had plenty of left, thanks to his guardian angel. All three bullets had miraculously missed his vital organs. Ian would have some ugly scars to show his grandchildren, but no real per-manent physical damage had been done.

Lily's parents had given Ian the back bedroom of their house. Lily had known that she could count on their unquestion-ing adherence to the country code of neighborliness. Her mother looked after him. Lily hadn't expected her to take such a shine to

Ian. But her third-eldest son had also been drafted into the war
and her second-eldest had been killed because of a Model T.
Though Ian was unable to speak, his smile spoke volumes. He
would reach for her mother's hand as she fussed over his pillows
and lay it next to his cheek. Lily's mother's eyes would well up
with tears then, and she would have to rush from the room. It
amused Lily that, without really realizing it, her mother had begun referring to Ian as her boy. *It's about time I checked on my boy in
the back*, she would say, excusing herself from the dinner table. She
made it her mission to fatten him up with corn chowder and rice
pudding—he was alarmingly underweight—and she sat with him
for hours in the afternoon, reading him articles from the *Barre
Times* and *Saturday Evening Post*. More than once, Lily had come
home from the library and caught the two of them dozing together, her mother snoring softly in the armchair next to his bed,
a bit of sewing in her lap; Ian lying on his back, his right hand
clutching the sleeve of her dress. Drunk on attention, like a baby
drunk on his mother's milk. Lily wondered: had Ian ever had the
undivided attention of anyone but Oren?

Lily made her way over to them. "I didn't bring enough food
for three," she said.

"Ian wanted to surprise you," Oren said.

"Well, it sure worked," Lily said. "I'm surprised." She ruffled Ian's bed-matted hair. "You tear any of those stitches out and
you'll have my mother after you. You boys had better tuck in to
what I've brought. I'm not all that hungry yet and, by the looks of
things up here, you've earned it. I'll make myself a sandwich before I head back to the library."

Oren opened up the hamper and handed Ian a sandwich.
They began eating in earnest. "Ian's bored to death," Oren said
between bites. "He thinks it would be good for him to get a little
exercise every day. Help the healing along. I won't let him lift anything heavy."

"He tell you all that?" Lily asked.

Oren stopped eating for a second. He and Ian exchanged one of their glances. "Well, not in so many words," Oren admitted.

Lily tried not to feel jealous of their secret world. She swatted at a deerfly with one of the napkins. "Is it ever hot up here!" she said.

"You don't have to stay, now that I've got my brother," Oren said.

"I didn't say I didn't want to help," Lily snapped. She stood and inspected the rafter the twins had been working on before lunch. It still needed another cross brace. She hauled an appropriate size timber off the pile and dragged it to the sawhorse.

"I guess it's time to get back to work," Oren laughed.

It didn't go well that afternoon. Lily was used to the rhythm of just her and Oren, of doing whatever he said. But Oren didn't have to tell Ian what to do—he knew already which tasks followed in what order—and Oren kept forgetting to let Lily in on the next step. Her frustration finally boiled over when both she and Ian bent to measure the same beam and knocked heads. Lily was so stunned by the blow that she fell backward and landed in a tuft of buttercups. She sat blinking for a moment and then burst into tears.

Oren stood by helplessly, a hammer dangling in his hand. Ian, rubbing his forehead, stooped to face her. His expression stopped her sobs. Just the right mixture of amusement and sympathy. He was trying to say something with his eyes. The strain of it was causing his mouth to twitch slightly. He held out his hand and she took it. He nodded in the direction of Oren.

"I don't understand," she snuffled. "That's the whole problem."

"Swim," Ian croaked.

Lily was caught completely off-guard. "What?" she said.

Oren dropped the hammer and crouched next to his brother.

"What did you say?"

"Swimmin'."

"You want to go swimming?" Lily giggled.

"Hot!" he said.

"Why not?" Oren laughed. "We could all use some cooling off."

"Are we ever going to catch hell for *this*," Lily said.

Lily was the first to shed her overalls and jump into the water. She couldn't remember the last time she had come to the
swimming hole—not since childhood. She paddled around the
middle of the pool, refusing to think about anything except staying afloat. She dove and stayed under as long as her breath would
allow. When she broke the surface, she watched Ian tug impatiently at his shirt collar while Oren unbuckled his overall straps
for him. Finally the two of them were naked. Oren cannonballed
into the water. Ian waded in the shallows, cautious of his bandages.

Lily thrilled at their daring. She would need to keep an ear
out for other visitors to the swimming hole. Imagine discovering
the town librarian in such a state! She also marveled at how easily
the three of them left their modesty, along with their rumpled
clothes, in a heap at the water's edge. Curious, she was so used to
Oren's body now, that the sight of Ian naked didn't embarrass her.
She and Oren had been lying with each other for months. She
loved making love with him. And they were getting pretty good at
it, she thought. It was lasting longer and longer now. There was
so much to it, much more than she would ever have imagined.

She watched Oren swing out over the pool and jack-knife
into the water—a heart-breakingly perfect dive. She glanced over
at Ian, who was splashing water onto himself, groaning slightly
with pleasure. Similar to Oren yet different: his arms and legs had

dwindled to nothing during the months he had been bedridden. So terribly thin that his chest seemed concave. When he caught her staring at him, he tried to splash her. She stuck her tongue out at him and dove underwater.

Oren eventually noticed that Ian was shivering and installed him on a big rock in the full sun. The two of them lay next to each other, drying off. Lily, still in the water, shivered herself. It was time she got out too; her fingertips had gone numb. She longed to join the twins on the rock. But she thought she heard children's voices in the woods. Whispers and laughter. She climbed out, toweled herself off on Oren's shirt and dressed quickly. She spread the damp shirt next to Oren on the rock, kissed him on the forehead and told him it was time she got back to town. He pleaded with her to stay a little longer—they were having such a nice time—but Lily was firm. "Get your brother back to the house," she said, "or my mother will skin you alive. And as far as she or anyone else is concerned, I've been at the library all afternoon—okay?"

"Lily swimmin'," Ian crowed.

"One word," Lily said, "and you'll wish you'd never gotten out of bed this morning."

A few days later, Oren declared it was time Ian moved out of the house. There was really no reason for him to be bedridden. And Ian didn't want to be a burden on Lily's family. Lily's mother remained unconvinced until Old Doc Perry confirmed Oren's prognosis during his next weekly visit. Ian's wounds were healing nicely, he said. A little exercise every day would probably give him an appetite. The lad just needed to be careful he didn't overexert himself and pop the stitches. Lily's mother relented, on condition that the two of them would come to dinner at the house every night. It was agreed, and Ian's army trunk was moved out of the back bedroom and into the caravan. Oren proved capable enough

of changing Ian's bandages, to the disappointment of every
Willard. They had all gotten used to having Ian around. Lily's
mother missed his unconcealed affection for her. Lily's father
missed beating him at chess. Lily's brothers missed rooting
around in his trunk for bullets and cigarettes.

What Lily missed, of course, was her nights of love-making
with Oren. She no longer had a good reason to spend two
evenings a week at the caravan. The sex, yes, she liked the physical
pleasure of it, the act of joining her body to Oren's. It made her
feel as though she belonged to someone else—in the same way
that her mother belonged to her father, her brothers belonged together in one loud boisterous pack, Ian belonged to Oren. But
when she thought about it, her nights at the caravan meant more
to her than that. She missed the seclusion. Away from the watch-
ful eyes of her parents, away from a house where her father had
never thought to install locks on any of the doors, Lily could feel
herself relaxing a little into the shape of the person she actually
was. It was while having dinner alone with Oren, giggling and
chewing with her mouth open, burping, that Lily first understood
the word privacy. And, she found, she missed spending time inside
the caravan itself. There was something comforting about how
small the interior was, how every object fit into the contours of
that space. The first time she and Oren made love among the pots
and pans, hammers and saws was also the first time she understood the meaning of intimacy.

Now she would have to wait, like everybody else, until her
wedding night to get these pleasures back. Or would she? A
thought struck her one night after the dishes were done. She told
her parents she was going up to bed early to read. But when she
got to her room, she did not pick up where she had left off in her
novel. She wedged a ladderback chair up under the doorknob. She
lay naked on top of the counterpane and let her fingers rove over
her own body to places where only Oren's fingers or tongue had

been. Her room grew smaller and smaller until it seemed that she existed only in a pinprick of light. And in her shudders, she discovered a new sort of privacy, a new intimacy that had been right under her own fingertips the entire time.

Summer waxed. The greens of the woodlot deepened. Thunderstorms hovered like headaches on the horizon. Tigerlilies sprang up once again along the Peacham Farm Road. Lily's thoughts turned to the matter of an engagement party. She had still not broached the subject with her mother. She was such a shy woman, her mother, one who did not go in for a lot of fuss—so much so, in fact, that she had been perfectly content to let Hallie organize her daughter's wedding. But Hallie was insistent on the matter of a party. The wedding had not yet been properly announced.

Lily was finishing the supper dishes with her mother one evening when she finally steeled her nerves and suggested a small gathering. Lily's mother pulled the plug in the sink and dried her hands on her apron. It was just a thought, Lily said, never mind. No, her mother said, people were probably expecting it. They could keep it small, Lily offered, just to say they had done it. Why not make it a barbecue and invite everybody? her mother said. In for a penny, in for a pound. There hadn't been a party at the Willard place in ten years—they were about due. The menu could be spit-roasted pig and a buffet of cold dishes with salads on the side. And wasn't the twins' birthday coming up soon? They could have cake, too—a surprise. Lily should pick up some nice stationery in town. They could write out the invitations together after supper, and Lily could post them before work the following morning.

Lily went to bed mystified. Just when you thought you knew someone.

Oren's birthday. She hadn't planned on Ian being back when she had first conceived of his present: a tune on her fiddle. She had been toiling haphazardly at the lesson book from the library, now long overdue. She had progressed from learning the strings to learning the notes you could play on each, to learning several tedious scales. She was finally teaching herself the notes to "For He's a Jolly Good Fellow." She had only ever intended to play it for Oren in private, after a nice dinner in the caravan with maybe a glass or two of wine to calm her nerves. Now there was a big party planned. Now she would have to play it for both of them— and the entire town, it seemed. This thought terrified her into wakefulness. She would have to begin practicing in earnest.

There wasn't really time, though, not until after the second mowing. It had been a wet summer so far; the hay crop was weedy and spare. Lily's father didn't dare to let it go any longer or it would rot on the stalk. So he mowed it in between storms and called all of his children into the fields to rake it into winnows. Lily suggested he use Ian as his hay cart driver. Ian was good with horses, and he was still unable to do any of the heavy lifting over at the building site. Lily's father agreed. He'd gladly take all the help he could get.

Oren was getting worried about Ian, Lily knew. Ian could only perform the tasks of a child—raking up sawdust after the builders, stacking the odd ends of wood, straightening nails, fetching water—and he was given to violent fits of temper about it. He wanted to be hammering and sawing, not just holding the lumber steady. When his frustration got to be too much for him, he would throw his straw hat down and stalk off, disappearing for hours.

Haying is an elaborate minuet. To winnow the cut grass into uniform rows, you need to establish a rhythm with your rake. It helps to hum a tune or chant a rhyme—perhaps one from your childhood—as you dip and sway across a mown field in time with the other rakers. To lift hay up into a cart you need a partner. You must bow low to scoop the golden grass into your tines. Your partner must swing his arms high, arcing his rake to meet yours in a single, fluid motion. Together you pirouette with your hay and fling it up into the cart. Meanwhile, the cart man must turn this way and that to weave it into sheaves, bundles that are easy to hoist into the loft once the cart has returned the barn. In a good mowing, not all of the hay you cut will fit into the loft. You leave great stacks of it behind in the fields, stacks that will weather out the winter with the heat of summer still trapped at the center even after the snow has melted and the top layers have all been stripped away.

Lily sang softly as she crossed the back pasture with her brothers. She tried her best to keep an eye on Ian—he was in the driver's seat of the cart, trundling just ahead, and she had promised Oren—but her mind kept wandering off in a different direction, waltzing across the hayfield in time to the song she was singing.

Lots of wine and dancing, slow waltzes through heavily perfumed air. Laughter like the jangle of a dozen bells. A simple white dress, much simpler than Hallie's, with lace cuffs and a long lace veil, both hand-tatted by her mother. Waltzing with Oren in a white room filled with white lilies—callas—white light cascading down from windows high up in the walls. Her new house.

Work ground to a halt. Lily's mother had arrived with the lemonade. Ian sidled up to Lily while she was mopping her neck with a handkerchief. He took the half-empty glass from her hand and gulped down the rest. Beneath a frayed straw hat, his face was beaded with sweat, and there were great salty rings under each of his arms. But he was grinning and his eyes sparkled. He seemed much happier today, with something useful to occupy him, something real. Without fully realizing it, Lily reached up and blotted at his forehead with her hanky. It seemed a completely natural thing to do—exactly how a fiancée would fuss over her betrothed. Except. Except that Ian would never be her husband. He would only look and smell and smile just like him. Lily tried to snatch her hand away. But Ian stopped it there on his cheek, grasping her wrist. And in that quick moment, barely a moment at all, Lily felt a jolt in her stomach, an odd mixture of emotions: sadness and frustration, suffocation and anger, acceptance. Longing—a deep aching sort of longing. She jerked her hand away. He smiled. She smiled back uncertainly.

"Still thirsty?" she asked.

He nodded.

"There's more," she said, grateful for an excuse to get away.

Later, she was hoisting hay into the cart with her youngest brother, thinking about this odd shock Ian had given her, when Dan, her father's gelded Belgian, whinnied and went down in his traces. The haycart lurched and nearly toppled on its side, half the hay cascading onto the ground. Lily quickly verified that Ian had not fallen—his stitches—though he looked badly shaken. She dropped her rake like the others and raced to see what had happened.

Dan had stumbled into a mole hole and twisted his right foreleg. Lily's father, along with some of the hands, unhitched him from Molly and waited for him to stop thrashing on the ground. Ian jumped from the seat of the cart and knelt at Dan's head. Lily's father barked at him to stand clear, but Ian ignored him and placed his hand on Dan's nose. The effect was instantaneous. Dan stopped kicking and lay still, though his belly huffed in terror and his eyes continued to roll. After gingerly examining the horse's foreleg, Lily's father declared that it was not broken. He had ripped up all of his tendons, though, and would be lame for life. Everyone clucked their tongues and shook their heads.

Dan was now useless as a workhorse. Lily's father stood. I'll just get my rifle, he said. He told one of his sons to run to the neighbor's in the meantime and borrow another horse for the rest of the afternoon. A storm was brewing; they needed to get the hay into the loft.

A wail went up. At first Lily thought it was Dan. But it wasn't. It was Ian.

"No," Ian moaned. "No gun."

Lily crouched next to him, placing a hand on his shoulder. "He's in terrible pain," she explained. "It's just the way of things, sometimes."

"No."

"Come away with me," Lily said. "We'll go over to the building site."

"Enough killing."

Silence in the hayfield. Silence as the farmfolk imagined what it must be like to be a foot soldier in Belgium, up to your waist in mud and water, piss and shit and blood. Facing death each and every morning after a sleepless night, stepping over cadavers half-buried in the trenches of Verdun, Messines and Ypres. Climbing over arms and legs and vacant staring eyes as you leave the trenches to engage in hand-to-hand combat. Killing, killing in the sulfuric haze of tear gas and gunsmoke. Creating more corpses as you make your way forward to the next trench half full of mud and water, piss and shit and blood.

Lily looked up at her father. "Can the leg be splinted?" she asked. "To get him onto his feet?"

"He's no good to me now," her father said.

"I know. But if he can stand, Ian and I can walk him over to my place and bandage the leg properly."

"You don't need another mouth to feed."

Lily turned to Ian. "Will you care for him? You might be able to ride him one day, but he'll never work again."

Ian nodded. His eyes brimmed with tears. "Thank you," he croaked.

"You won't be so grateful when you're cleaning up after him," Lily said.

To ease their embarrassment, the menfolk got busy splinting Dan's leg and wrapping it tightly in Ian's shirt. By the time the horse was on his feet again, another gelding had been brought from the neighboring farm. Lily and Ian began their slow walk back to her property, waiting patiently for Dan to hobble across the field on three legs. As soon as they were safely out of everyone's sight, Ian grabbed Lily and hugged her close. "I want to take care of him," he said. His first real sentence. She dangled there in his arms, her feet not touching the ground, squeezing him back, smelling him, understanding.

She got more of an opportunity to practice her song as soon as haying was over. The walls of her new house were going up now. Raising them required the help of hired men from town, just as she remembered from childhood. This left her free at lunch time. Instead of turning up at the building site, though, she once again began hiding herself away in the milk house during her two-hour break from the library. She knew closing it was an outrageous liberty—she had no authority to adjust a public facility's hours of operation to her own personal whims—and she promised herself she would toe the line in the fall, once the school-children returned and she had more to keep her busy. Not that she liked practicing much. The problem with learning to play a musical instrument, she decided, was the learning part—which was no fun at all. She knew it would one day give her great pleasure to be able to play music. But when was that day? And how long would it take her to get there?

She was seated at her music stand fretting about all this when Ian burst in. She had been running through her high scales to limber up her fingers. She never seemed able to hit the crescendoing "fellow" notes in "For He's a Jolly Good Fellow" because her fingers weren't up to both the stretch and the pressure necessary to pin them down. Suddenly there was Ian, carrying an empty pitcher. She stopped playing. He stared at her, dumbfounded.

"Milk," he said, holding up the pitcher. "Lunch milk."

Lily set the fiddle in her lap, deflated. Her surprise was ruined—well, at least half of it. She waved him in and motioned for him to shut the door. "Can you keep a secret?" she asked. Ian nodded solemnly. "I'm teaching myself how to play 'For He's a Jolly Good Fellow' for Oren. Want to hear?" Ian nodded again. Lily played what she could of the song, stopping at the screeching notes. "That's about as far as I've gotten," she said. "What do you think?"

Ian set his pitcher down. He dragged one of the full milk cans over next to her and motioned for her to hand him the fiddle. He held it for a moment, weighing it, running his hands up its neck, peering into its F-holes. "Oren made it for me," Lily said. "For my last birthday. Beautiful, isn't it?" He nodded. He placed it under his chin. Lily handed him the bow. He set it to the strings. His version of "For He's a Jolly Good Fellow" sounded nothing like Lily's. It was light as angel food cake, playful. When he got to the part that was giving Lily trouble, he teased the high notes out of the strings in a way that made Lily laugh, as if the fiddle were singing the song and poking a little fun at her in the process.

"I'll never be able to do that," she said.

Ian patted his lap. It took Lily a moment to understand that he wanted her to sit there. She hesitated, but he insisted until she got up and perched on his knee. He made her take the fiddle under her own chin, but held both of his hands over hers. Together they gripped the fiddle's neck in their left hands and the bow in their rights. Long thick fingers, tanned a chestnut brown with wisps of fine bleached hair on the knuckles; broad pink nails, chipped, with light pink half-moons at their bases. Oren's fingers. Ian's breath was sweet like hay—like Oren's. She tried to ignore that warming feeling in her belly, the one she got when Oren kissed her in the caravan. Her body was merely confused by the familiar hands, the familiar breath, the familiar lap. How could she be blamed if this sort of intimacy with her brother's twin felt completely familiar, totally natural?

Ian nodded for her to begin. She refocused on her own fingers and started to play. She could feel his chin digging into her shoulder as he watched. Every so often he corrected the placement of her fingertips on the fret or the angle at which she cocked the bow over the bridge. This made all the difference in the world. With his help, she played her way through the entire song without stopping. It didn't sound anything like his version, of course. But it did sound better than before.

"Thanks," Lily whispered.

"Welcome," Ian whispered back.

They sat like that a moment longer, with Lily on his lap and his arms around her. She thought she heard Oren calling for Ian off in the distance. Or was it just her overactive imagination again, like the laughter of children in the woods? Lily stood and smoothed out her dress. Ian grinned and opened the can he had been sitting on. He filled his pitcher with ice cold milk. He winked at Lily, before slipping out of the milk house. She stood, staring at the inside of the door.

Ian crossing the yard to his brother, the two of them children again. Ian dropping the pitcher of milk. Running, running in a complete panic. Oren in the orchard. Not calling Ian's name. Silent. Silent and lying beneath the old crab apple. Asleep? Staring up at the sky through a latticework of branches?

A cold shiver ran the length of Lily's spine. Mercifully, the milk house door had become solid maple again. *You see more than you let on.*

She was not a seer.

She stood and peered out its one tiny pane. No sign of either Pritchard. They must have crossed the road together. Or Ian had merely climbed the knoll to the site by himself. She sat once again before her stand. There was still time to practice what Ian had taught her.

The morning of the party dawned clear. And though the paper said it would stay clear, Lily knew by bread-making time that troubled skies lay ahead. It was going to be one of those days when nothing went according to plan. The bread hadn't risen, for example, because the yeast had died. There weren't enough eggs to make both another batch and the surprise birthday cake unless Lily went to town. This meant that Ian had to stop helping Oren at the new house to mind the spit. Lily's father, who had laid the pit the night before, had not counted on such a heavy dew and, as a result, the coals weren't nearly hot enough when it came time to remove the pig from its brine and truss it up. Her father had had to stoke the fire back up. Now, unless the spit was watched constantly, the pig might scorch in the flames. He could not watch the spit himself; he and Lily's brothers were racing to get the corn chopped and into the barn before the crows got most of it. Unfortunately, Lily had intended to lower the hem on her only decent dress while she was watching the spit. Now she was going to town for eggs. And her mother was too busy making the side dishes to hem her dress. So no one was doing what had originally been planned.

The stress finally got to Lily when she returned from town with the eggs. She went out to inspect the pig's progress, saw that it was a long way from done, and burst into tears.

"What?" Ian croaked in alarm.

"It'll never be ready in time," she snuffled. "I wanted everything to be perfect."

Ian laughed his musical laugh (one of the few traits he did not share with Oren; Oren's laugh was more of a quiet chuckle); he took her into his arms and gave her a reassuring hug. "You're perfect, Lily," he said. "Don't worry." She laughed, too; she couldn't help it. Ian's hugs always made her feel better.

She noticed Hallie wafting across the lawn. Hallie was in her best party dress, and she was at least two hours early for the party. "Damn!" Lily muttered, pushing Ian away. She was overcome by a fresh wave of panic. The event ahead became real to her in that instant. The barbecue. Her song. She hadn't had time to practice. "Hallie!" she squeaked, attempting to mask her dismay.

"Congratulations, you two!" Hallie crowed, throwing her arms first around Lily, then Ian. "Gosh," she said, "you're thin as a rail, Oren. Lily must be running you ragged to get her house finished."

"That's, um, Ian," Lily said, tucking a lock of damp, smoky hair behind her ear. "Oren's twin brother. He was offering me some badly needed moral support. You knew, Hallie, that he was back from the war?"

"Shame on you for never once bringing him by the house to introduce us," Hallie said. "Then again, I've barely seen *you* since your dress got finished. Good thing I have my church sewing circle or I wouldn't know anything about the goings-on up here."

Pure Hallie, thought Lily. Bundling together disapproval of Lily's manners, disappointment with her temporary lapse of contact, and dismay at not hearing about Ian's existence from her first, all in one amazing breath. "Well then, it's high time the two of you met," Lily said, blazing ahead—what else could possibly go awry?—"Ian Pritchard, meet Hallie Burke. Johnson, I mean. Sorry, Hallie, I always forget to use your married name."

"Pleased to meet you, Ian."

Ian smiled and nodded. He grabbed hold of Lily's sleeve. An awkward silence followed. Lily couldn't very well explain about Ian's speech loss now, in front of him.

"Speaking of your husband," Lily said, "where is he? Up at the site with Oren? Feels like I haven't seen him in ages, either."

"He had to send his regrets," Hallie said. "He's been working like a dog at that bank of his. He gets these terrible headaches—migraines, Doc Perry calls them—ones that lay him out flat in bed."

"How awful," Lily said. "Be sure to send him my best. We'll make a plate."

"Yes," Hallie said. "Meantime, Ian'll just have to be my escort—unless he's already been snatched up."

Ian shook his head no. He colored slightly and looked down at his boots.

"Excellent," Hallie said. "That pig needs turning, by the way."

As it turned out, Hallie was a godsend. A mere glimpse of Lily's frazzled mother and her chaotic kitchen was all Hallie needed to claim she was there to help, in spite of her good dress. Lily's mother did not object; in fact, she stopped mixing cake batter only long enough to hand Hallie an apron. Hallie insisted Lily sit on the back porch and finish hemming her dress. Meanwhile, she had Ian help her arrange the tables on the back lawn in a more social configuration. These she set with fresh linens as well as flowers cut from the good bed. (Lily managed to pull her aside long enough on one of her many trips back to the kitchen to explain about Ian. Hallie took the news in stride; she could talk enough for the both of them, she said. Were there any more teacups besides those that were out?) She seemed to be everywhere at once: folding napkins into fans, checking on the pig, slicing hardboiled eggs for potato salad.

"Where on earth is Oren?" she cried suddenly.

"He must still be up at the new house," Lily said.

"Well, go and get him, for heaven's sake. Your guests will be arriving any minute."

"Maybe Ian could fetch him," Lily said. "I've still got a few odds and ends to tie up." She was thinking about her tune and how she hadn't had a second to practice.

Hallie wouldn't hear of it. Ian needed to help her get that pig off the spit—if there was any hope of eating it. Now run along.

Lily found Oren in the skeleton of the new house. He was showing her eldest brother and his wife around. They were on the second level, wandering the catwalk planking. Oren was pointing out where their bedroom would be, where Lily's sewing room would be, where Ian's room would be. Lily greeted her brother and sister-in-law with a hug. She hated to interrupt the tour, she said, but if Oren wanted to wash up he had probably better get himself across the road.

Hallie had stationed herself at the front door with Ian to greet Lily's guests. She was laughing and chatting with everyone, sending the womenfolk around back to deposit the dishes and desserts they had brought to the buffet table, getting Ian to serve the menfolk with either a glass of punch or something harder from Lily's father's liquor cabinet in the parlor. She kissed Oren hello on the cheek and assured Lily everything was just fine. They should both get themselves changed. Lily really needed to do something about that hair.

Lily sat in the bathtub and stewed. It was small of her to resent Hallie for having saved the day. After all, Hallie had done it for her. But why did she have to be so damn perfect all the time? No one cooked better, no one sewed a straighter seam, no one set a better table. Lily frowned. It wasn't as though she wanted to excel at any of these things; she just didn't care to be reminded that she didn't. She splashed water onto her back. She sighed. In truth, she was also irritated by Hallie's outrageous flirting. Hallie was a married woman for Pete's sake—to the town banker—how did she get away with it? Clutching Ian by the arm wherever she went, introducing him to all and sundry, whispering behind his back that it was his birthday, that there would be cake later; that he had lost his voice, poor thing, in the war to save the world from the Kaiser. And Ian was quite happy to trot around behind her like a puppy.

And this is where Ian's room will be.

The barbecue was in full swing when she finally stepped out onto the back porch. The women were laughing and gossiping around Hallie's elegant tables. The men were playing horseshoes and pretending not to gossip in the orchard. Standing on the bottom step was Oren. He was shiny from a vigorous scrubbing, wearing his good shirt, beaming up at her. And suddenly this pear-shaped day righted itself for Lily. She remembered what she was here for: to celebrate her engagement to this man, this handsome, talented, intelligent, wonderful man. This man who had loved her since he was nine years old.

He held out his hand for her. She took it. And together they navigated the tables, making their hellos, accepting everyone's congratulations. Lily had never felt more grown-up. They all liked Oren. Oren's brother was a war hero. They made a handsome couple, the two of them. She looked beautiful in her dress. They were in love.

Some evenings, people are in the mood for a party. It doesn't happen all that often, but when it does it's magic. The weather has to be right. Those who turn up will have had a decent day of cribbing corn. And it helps if you've had a pull or two off the jug and won a game of horseshoes. Then you can take yourself out of your daily life and enjoy the company of others—your neighbors, folks who all struggle with the same weather, who enjoy the same sunset, the same pig roasted to perfection, the same gossip and fireflies, potato salad, horseshoes and corn liquor.

In fact, Lily was enjoying herself so much her mother had to remind her to bring out the cake. She grabbed Hallie and dragged her to the kitchen. Together they lit the candles, giggling in anticipation. Lily uncased her fiddle and tuned it up. Hallie followed her with the cake to where the twins were seated. Silence in the orchard. The twins glanced at each other, then turned their full attention to Lily. She took a deep breath—she hadn't had a single moment to practice all day—and began to play. She made a mistake or two. But no one really noticed because they had all begun to sing along. Oren's eyes were brimming with tears. Ian's sparkled with mischief—he had kept Lily's secret, as he'd promised. Both sets of eyes said, thank you dear Lily, this is our dream come true: family and friends, a place to live, a place to belong, someone to love. Lily had begun to learn their language.

Applause and laughter. Blow out the candles, boys. Make a wish!

When she finished, Oren jumped up to hug her. "I thought you had shoved it away in a closet," he said.

"Sorry I'm not very good yet," she said. "I've been kind of busy with one thing and another."

He cupped her face in his hands. He kissed her, right there in front of everyone. More laughter and applause, and a toast to the two of them. Suddenly, the first resonant chords of a lively tune. Lily and Oren whirled around. Ian had taken up her fiddle. He began to play a jig, slowly at first but picking up speed as people around him began to clap, then dance. Ian jumped up onto the table. *Careful of those stitches!* The crowd roared their approval. After the jig, he went into a waltz. Soon everyone was dancing. One of the neighbors, who had brought his banjo (in case just such a thing might happen—it wasn't out of the question at a barbecue on the prettiest night of the year) joined Ian among the dirty plates and coffee cups. A harmonica player emerged from the fray, then someone with a guitar. People squared up for a reel.

Lily begged off—there were tables to clear and dishes to wash—but her neighbors would hear none of it. She and Oren were swept up and carried off. They were partners for the first couple of dances, but then well-wishers cut in. It didn't matter. Lily was happy to dance with anyone, twirling and clapping, swinging whichever partner was closest by, laughing and laughing, losing track of time.

When she stopped to catch her breath, she scanned the crowd for Oren. He was sitting with her father, playing a game of chess, sharing a mason jar of dandelion wine. She looked for Ian, who had stopped to rest his fingers a few reels before. Hallie had asked him to dance. Now he had disappeared. Lily looked for Hallie. She had also disappeared. She took a few deep breaths. Ian had probably walked Hallie home. It was the gentlemanly thing to do. Anyway, it was none of her business. She strode with purpose toward Oren and her father. She asked her fiancé to dance. He was more than happy to oblige.

After the last good-byes, they walked back to the caravan together. Their way was lit by fireflies and the moon. It was deep into the night now, and bats darted around them in the blue air. They made their way slowly, drunk on dancing and dandelion wine. Lily giggled when she stumbled over a root. Oren hugged her a little closer and whispered, Shh, you'll wake Ian.

Where Ian's room will be.

They kissed at the back door of the caravan for a good long time. But finally Lily broke it off. She could feel herself pressing into Oren's thigh each time he stroked her breasts through her dress, feel the dampness between her own legs and the incredible heat there. "I'd better get back," she groaned.

"No, wait," Oren said, his voice rasping. "I'll never be able to sleep. Couldn't we—?"

"Here?"

"Why not? Ian sleeps like the dead."

Lily giggled again. Oren clamped his hand over her mouth. She bit his thumb. This caused him to yelp. When he loosened his grip, she let his thumb slip into her mouth. She began licking the salt off. He moaned softly. Lily added his index finger.

"Step out of your drawers," Oren whispered.

Oren took his fingers out of Lily's mouth. She hiked up her dress and dropped her underwear to the dirt. Thank goodness she hadn't had time to bother with a corset. Oren stepped forward and fumbled in the folds of fabric and petticoats with his dampened fingers until he found the heat he was seeking. Lily saw stars. Her legs buckled, but Oren caught her. He leaned her against the steps of the back door. Then he placed those fingers into his own mouth, even damper than before. He placed them into Lily's. After that, more stars—the entire Milky Way peeking through the pines, revolving overhead, washing away in a river of nectar and salt.

"Stay the night," Oren whispered when they were kissing again. "I'll wake you before dawn. No one at the house will ever know."

"What about Ian?" she said.

"He won't care."

"That's just plain stupid."

"I want to sleep with you, Lily," Oren said. He kissed her again.

"All right, but just for a little while," Lily said. "Until you fall asleep."

Oren led her inside, where it was completely dark. Lily was afraid she would knock a saw or kettle off the wall and wake Ian. But Oren knew the interior of the caravan by heart and led her to the bed without mishap.

Ian was sleeping there. She could hear him breathing.

She had never thought about the sleeping arrangements. Or if she had, she had always imagined Ian in the upper bunk where the twins had slept as children. But of course he couldn't sleep up there. That would be impossible, what with his bandages and stitches. But clearly Oren wasn't sleeping there either; the cupboard doors weren't folded down. Then again, why should he? It was cramped, a space comfortable only for nine-year-olds. The twins had slept together all their lives . . .

"No," Lily said. "I'm going back."

"Shh," Oren said. "There's plenty of room."

"That's not the point."

"There is no point, Lily."

Lily couldn't see Oren in the dark. But she could sense him, there, all around. She loved him, and she knew there were parts of him, important parts of his personality and character, parts that she loved when she told herself that she loved him, that lived outside his body. He would never truly exist without his brother. He had pointed out Ian's room when he was showing off their new house. Of course Ian would have a room, of course he would be living with them after they got married. Oren's "I" would always be mixed up with his "we." But he loved her, she knew that. He wanted to marry her. And tonight he wanted to sleep with her.

"You first," she said. "I'm not sleeping in the middle."

"Thank you," he said, and began to undress.

And as she lay there, drifting off to sleep, Lily saw how things would be. She would wake well before dawn and sneak back to the house. She would remove her shoes out on the front lawn and tiptoe up the stairs to her room, avoiding the squeaky boards. And she would pretend to wake in her own bed, greet the day as the properly raised girl her mother believed her to be. But as she lay in the twins' bed, in between wakefulness and dreaming, she had a waking dream about her wedding. She could see it all clearly: there would be dancing. Dancing with wild abandon around a bonfire, shadows and light flickering on naked skin, the surrounding hemlocks, the clapboard sides of a caravan. Dancing to lively fiddle music and laughter, dancing to entice the rain to come. What other celebration could she imagine? She had spoken her vows as soon as she had undressed and climbed into this bed.

4

FAR TO GO

[1 9 2 1]

IN THE RAW TWILIT AIR OF MARCH, Lily could still feel a tingle where, earlier that afternoon, Hallie had slapped her. It would snow later, she knew. A sugar snow. She lifted her fingers to her cheek. Actual pain had subsided within a moment or two. The slap hadn't been hard enough to raise a welt, but wonder about it had lingered well beyond the handprint—until now on the slushy plod home from the library. Gray, gray all around. The doldrums of winter. Spring a far-away dream.

She should have kept her mouth shut about Hallie's husband. If she had feigned surprise at the news of his sudden departure, her cheek would not be tingling now. When Hallie had burst into the library and burst into tears, she should have simply dragged her into the back room for a cup of tea. Hallie had come to Lily for comfort—not for the truth. Certainly not for a detailed explanation of *why* her husband had emptied their bank account, packed up his shiny new Ford in the middle of the night, and driven off for parts unknown. How could Hallie have been expected to see the connection between her husband's sudden departure and his repeated failure to get a favorite hunting beagle to mount a neighbor's purebred bitch?

Lily reddened at the thought. *You see more than you think.* Her encounter with Mme. LeTourneau on this very road. For

Lily, the signs were all around in nature: some that foretold the future, others that revealed the past, still others that explained the present. It was like walking into the library, opening up a book and reading what was there. Yet, no one else but she ever seemed to decipher them—or notice, even, that they were there. Why? In any case, Lily's mother had chided her throughout her childhood for her silly notions. She had learned over time to keep them to herself. So what had suddenly compelled her *now* to try to make Hallie read the signs about her husband?

"How could you say something so hateful?" Hallie had hissed. Then she had hauled off and slapped Lily, right there in front of all the old-timers. "Don't you be spreading such a vicious rumor around town or I will make you regret the day you were born."

Lily stopped walking. She stood in the middle of the Peacham Farm Road and drew in several deep breaths. Metallic scent of snow, bitter taste of mud. She sighed. At least it was Friday. She wouldn't have to face returning to the library for two whole days, now. She made a vow. Here forward, she *would* hold her tongue. She would limit her opinions to matters concerning her new house on the hill, Mount Mansfield under its eiderdown quilt, and her horses watering themselves at a break in the ice in the brook. She could only hope spring was around the next bend in the road.

When she reached the paddock fence of her property, she whistled. She waited for the horses to file up the path and nuzzle her for sugar cubes. They had four horses now and she loved each of them ferociously, having rescued them all from slaughter. She had paid next to nothing—thanks to their obvious imperfections. The younger of the two mares was sway-backed; the elder so old she was toothless. Dan, the gelded Belgian she had saved from her father's rifle, would always limp. The stallion, though magnificently proportioned, didn't seem interested in mating with females. Same as that hired beagle. Same as Hallie's husband.

What bothered Lily most about Hallie's slap was the nagging notion that it was, in itself, a sign—one meant for her, one she couldn't yet interpret. *You're doing it again.* She doled out sugar cubes and put the matter out of her head. She wasn't in the mood for omens at the moment. Right now, she was enjoying life for what it was: she loved her job, she loved her husband, she loved her home, she loved her horses. She checked the mailbox once her pockets were empty and stopped to admire her house. Her spirits lifted instantly.

They called it The Knoll. Part Greek temple, part New England Colonial, part Southern plantation—it defied description, really. To be sure, it borrowed from Mr. Pritchard's copy of *Payne's Encyclopedia of Rural Residences.* Lily recognized design elements from The Kent, The Somerset and The Wellington. But there the comparison ended. The objective of those pattern-book houses was to contrast themselves against the landscape, tame it, defy it. Oren's house wanted to work with its surroundings, spreading itself out on the knoll, wrapping around it to accommodate the rocky ground's irregular rises and falls, jutting out with spectacular columnar porches wherever this wasn't possible. Many of the enormous rooms inside were connected by small staircases rather than corridors because so few of them were built on the same level. Then again, almost every room boasted a breathtaking view, thanks to unusually tall windows that brought the outside inside and suffused the interior with delicious light. All of the furniture was simple and spare, built by hand. Nothing on the walls. Oren had insisted that the house's chief decoration be space. Lily thought it beautiful. But she knew there was gossip about it around town. People lived and died in Cabot Fields because they liked square boxes and right angles.

She started up the drive, a neatly shoveled path that took its time (and several turns) getting to the front steps. They still hadn't managed to build a horse barn yet. The Pritchard caravan was never parked long enough at The Knoll for one to get raised. This was probably a good thing; it meant the brothers' carpentry business was booming. Luckily the horses didn't seem to mind their unorthodox existence, huddling at night under a makeshift lean-to beneath the hemlocks.

Something delicious was roasting for dinner. One of Oren's famous chickens. The aromas of garlic and rosemary greeted her at the front door—as did three cats. Lily shouted that she was home, then knelt to scratch each cat behind the ears. One of the twins shouted back that they were in the kitchen. Even after a year of marriage, it was impossible for Lily to distinguish which brother was which from their voices alone. Lily hung her cloak on a peg by the door and made her way to the back of the house.

Oren was at the oven basting. Ian was seated at the kitchen table, peeling potatoes. An open bottle of red wine sat expectantly on the chopping block with three goblets perched next to it. There was always wine. Lily didn't like to think how they got it, now that Prohibition was on. The benefits of living close to the Canadian border, she hoped—especially with the connections of itinerant carpenters. "My heroes!" she exclaimed, kissing the top of Ian's head and then kissing Oren on the lips. "I'm absolutely starving."

"Well, there's another good hour before this tough old buzzard is ready," Oren said. "Will a sandwich tide you over? There's still some roast beef in the ice box."

Lily grabbed a carrot from a freshly washed bunch of them drying in a colander. "Oh, this'll do," she said, "—and a big glass of wine."

"Pour it, Lily," Ian said. "We waited for you."

Lily did exactly that, handing them each a goblet. She raised hers in a toast. They both followed suit. This was one of Lily's favorite moments of the day: the last light of the afternoon streaming through the window over the sink, a kettle chuffing on the back burner ready to parboil potatoes, carrots in a colander in need of peeling, the three of them smiling and smiling.

"Tough day among the tomes?" Oren asked, after they had all taken a sip.

"Hey, why are you two home so early?" Lily asked, changing the subject. She loved this—the three of them in the kitchen, cooking and sipping wine, swapping stories—she loved it too much to invite Hallie and her unexpected slap to dinner. The whole town would be gossiping about her husband's sudden departure by morning. The twins would hear all about it soon enough.

I will make you regret the day you were born.

No, Lily would much rather hear about the twins' day. She found it fascinating, that they built houses out of pattern books, yet they had never succeeded in building any two that were identical. People had very specific—and highly individual—notions of what would make a comfortable home. Some needed the kitchen ell on the opposite side of the house, some need an indoor bathroom, some needed fireplaces upstairs as well as down. And the more the twins got to know a family, the more changes they began to make to the house's design—not necessarily to accommodate what the family said was home, but what they really meant by it.

"We were back at The Knoll before school let out," Ian said. "Reverend Higgins doesn't know whether he's afoot or on horseback. He's changed his mind three times about that goddamn pulpit. Now he wants it in maple and we haven't got any."

"It was too late to get to the lumberyard in Danville. So we just made all the repairs we could to the ceiling," Oren said. "But plastering is slow work and you have to wait for one section of molding to dry before you can start on the next or you make a goddamn mess of it. So we knocked off early."

"And what did the good Reverend have to say about that?"

"Nothing much," Oren laughed. "He was taking tea in the rectory with Old Lady Blanchard at the time. Besides, he's tickled pink about the new pews we carved for him. He claims he's going to convince the Elders to approve that new steeple. So keep your fingers crossed."

"Or better yet, say a prayer," Ian said.

The three of them laughed. The twins had never attended an actual church service in their lives—apart from Oren's marriage to Lily—though they had carved countless saints and crucifixes over the years. Mr. Pritchard had severed all relations with the Father, Son and Holy Ghost when his wife died in childbirth.

Lily proposed that Ian give her a fiddling lesson, in the waiting time before supper. Ian happily agreed. They could work on the new piece, he said, the one they were planning to debut at the Grange's Sugar-On-Snow Dance the following night. Oren promised he would fetch them as soon as the food was on the table. There was nothing he hated more than dried-out chicken. Lily munched carrots as she followed Ian to the music room. The cats all trailed behind, which made her laugh. Animals adored Ian, for some reason. The Pied Piper of Cabot Fields.

The music room was originally meant to be Lily's sewing room. But she hated sewing almost as much as she hated cooking and did as little of both as possible. Admittedly, the twins were hard on their work clothes. Barely a day went by without one of them losing a shirt button or ripping a hole in their overalls. But they had been repairing their own clothes all their lives. Carving chess pieces had made their fingers nimble at threading a needle. Lily had set up her music stand in the bay window, where the Singer should have gone. She loved her fiddle. And she continued to learn how to read music from that overdue library book. But her real musical progress was thanks to Ian, who was teaching her how to play by ear.

They were working on a duet at the moment. It was a complicated waltz, the most difficult piece Lily had ever attempted. She had grown skilled at playing harmony to some of Ian's livelier jigs. But this was entirely different. Ian was meant to play one melody in a major key while she played another in minor. In this waltz, she wasn't following Ian; she was playing against him. The result was yet a third melody, plaintive and hopeful, when it worked out. Unfortunately, it rarely worked out.

They began. As Lily played, her mind drifted with the notes. The two melodies sounded like a conversation, two voices—a man's and a women's—two lovers quarreling and then making up. Voices. Ian's speech had improved so much. It had not been clear upon his return from the war whether he would ever speak again. He had broken through the barrier of silence, though, that afternoon of swimming. But progress had been slow after that. A word here, a phrase there. The horses. The horses had somehow made a huge difference. Ian had spoken his first real sentences the day Dan had gone down in his traces. *I want to take care of him.* And so he had, feeding him and brushing him, untangling his mane, walking him for an hour every afternoon to build enough strength in his leg to saddle him. It was on Dan that Ian had first begun to practice his speech. He would ride around the property for hours. Lily wondered what he said to the Belgian during these rides. She imagined him talking about the war, sharing, at last, some of the horrors that had rendered him speechless. Whatever it was worked. Every time he returned to the corral, his ability to communicate with words improved a little. Ian never spoke to Lily about the war. He never spoke at all when he was alone with Oren.

Ian stopped playing and set his fiddle in his lap. Lily's bow skittered to a halt on her bridge. "Now what's the matter?" she asked. Practice had seemed effortless for a change; she thought she had been playing beautifully.

"You keep getting tangled up in my part," he said.

"What are you talking about? I was playing mine the whole time."

"No you weren't. You were in a world of your own. And you started copying what I was doing. You're not good enough yet, Lily, to play without concentrating. You still have to focus all your attention on it."

"I liked you better when you couldn't scold me," Lily giggled.

"Well do you want to get better or not?" Ian said, grinning.

"You're going to have to show me the tricky part of that second verse again," Lily said. "I promise to give it my undivided attention."

Ian moved the fiddle off his lap. Lily climbed into it and cued up her own fiddle. Long thick fingers with chipped nails and a smattering of blond hair on the knuckles. She wondered if Oren and Ian had the same fingerprints. He took her through the movement a phrase at a time, playing it first for her, then guiding her hands as she played it afterward. Several tries later, she was able to play her part of the song on her own.

Not undivided. That warm feeling in the pit of her stomach was there, just like the first time she had sat in his lap in the milk house. Back then, she remembered thinking that she was merely confusing him chemically with Oren—his size, his hands, his smell. Now, she wondered. The more she had gotten to know him, the more she realized how similar the two of them were, she and Ian, how much they had in common: their love of fiddling and making music, their love of horses and kittens and all animals, their unquestioning—almost blind—devotion to Oren.

She was playing Ian's part again. "Damnit!" she cried. "I almost had it that time." She looked up and saw that Oren was leaning in the doorway, arms crossed, watching them. She smiled. He smiled back. "Supper's ready," he said.

"Thank God," Ian said, "my legs are falling asleep."

—

Lily attacked both her dinner and the chessboard with gusto. The three of them had taken to playing triangular chess while they ate. Oren had invented the game when Lily had objected to being left out of matches between the twins. He had carved a clever triangular board inlaid with black and white marble triangles, large enough to accommodate three sets of chessmen— golden maple for Lily, dark cherry for Ian, and light birch for himself. The object of the game was the same as ordinary chess. But the pieces had slightly different moves now to accommodate the triangular board. Checking an opponent could be a collaborative effort between the other two players and, in the process, alliances often formed and dissolved with dizzying rapidity. At the moment, Lily was winning. But not by much. Oren and Ian were mounting a rather worrisome offensive.

"I'm on to you," she cried, repositioning a rook to protect her queen.

"Better open another bottle of wine," Ian muttered, capturing one of the pawns in her defensive line.

"She won't see the bottom of another glass," Oren said, standing. This upset the black-and-white kitten that had crawled into his lap to lick his empty plate. Oren made for the cupboard where the wine was secretly stowed. The kitten skittered under the table. Over the next hour, Oren's prediction turned out to be correct. Lily was checkmated by Ian. But the effort had significantly weakened his forces. After that, Oren made short work of him. Ian demanded a rematch, but Lily begged off. She needed to get up early the next morning, she said, to help her mother bake pies for the Grange dance. She and Oren did the supper dishes while Ian played his fiddle for them. They all decided to turn in early.

"I'll be up in a minute," Lily said, making her way to the

front of the house. She opened the door quietly and slipped outside. These days, she was in the habit of filling her lungs with
fresh air before bed. It was cold out on the front porch. Sugar
snow. Her eldest brother had been anticipating it for weeks. He
needed the sap to start running soon or his maple sugaring season
would be a disaster. She took ten deep breaths, hugging herself to
keep warm. Through a break in the trees, she could see the lights
of Cabot Fields down in the valley. But when she exhaled, the
town disappeared in a puff of vapor.

Back inside, she bolted the door. She had begun to lock both
the front and back doors at night. Though Ian's shell shock had
more or less abated, he had a tendency to sleepwalk. Sometimes
he would wander into their room in the middle of the night and
stand by their bed, as though he were guarding it. More than
once, Lily or Oren had woken the next morning to find him out
with the horses. It was too cold now for him to be wandering
around the property naked.

Lily hitched her shawl a little more tightly around her neck.
Though it had snowed heavily during the night, the day had
dawned clear, and the early morning air was so frosty it caught in
her throat. The perfect day for boiling syrup—if the temperature
crept above freezing. By mid-afternoon the sap would be running
so well in her brother's maple grove that it would overflow the
galvanized buckets. The first run of the season. Lily pressed on. If
she finished early enough with her mother, she might be able to
catch the last of the collecting. There were only a handful of days
each spring when the conditions were right for making syrup: a
storm and a freeze followed by a thaw. There was the first run in
March, then maybe a second in April. If you were lucky, you
might get a frog run, named after the spawning of the peepers in
the bog. It was all over by the budding of the trees—the sap got

too bitter—though some tried to boil it in desperation, batting away the new insects attracted to the sweet steam—hence the name moth run. By then it was spring.

Her mother's kitchen was stifling. The oven had been going since breakfast; half a dozen pies were already cooling in the safe in the summer kitchen. She mopped her brow with her sleeve and bent back to her work. Would it ever end? Lily was rolling out fresh crust while her mother crimped the edges of two more apple pies. She watched her mother vent the tops with the Willard family pattern. She wanted nothing more than to be outside with the twins. Little hope of that now. They were only half finished. They were making extra pies for the men who were maple sugaring. Always good to have pie onhand in the sugarhouse. Amazing how much pie a farmer could eat, if the crust was good—with every meal, including breakfast, and most likely with coffee in between. She forced herself to focus on what her mother was saying.

Hallie's misfortune. Hallie's husband had been having an affair with some divorcée from St. Johnsbury, according to town gossip. His mistress liked to live well, they said, eating out every night, nice clothes, trips into Burlington to see the shows. Over time, this had put quite a strain on his finances, and he had begun to take money from the tills. The bank would probably never have found out—Hallie's husband had always intended to pay the money back—but area farmers had been borrowing pretty heavily against the coming harvest (it was going to be a good year, according to the Almanac, so they were buying the new equipment they needed now) and the bank had suddenly come up short. Hallie's husband had been let go. He had decided to leave town, to avoid the shame of having to face anyone. Apparently, slipping away in the middle of the night had been easy enough for him to do, since he and Hallie were now keeping separate bedrooms. Speculation was that he had moved in with the other woman— though Hallie claimed she didn't know where he was. In any case,

Hallie planned to keep on living at the house. But she was going to seek a legal annulment, first thing. It was the only sensible thing to do—

Wasn't there anything else they could talk about? Lily asked.

Lily's mother smiled conspiratorially. Well, if you can keep a secret, she said. The wife of Lily's eldest brother had just confided in her that she was pregnant with her first. She was already about four months along—wasn't that nice? Lily's mother was planning to bleach some white wool and knit a set of booties for the baptism. Of course, it would be just as easy for her to knit two sets if Lily ever wanted to share similar news of her own.

Lily wanted to scream. Her mother had been hinting for weeks now that it was time to have a baby. She didn't want one. She liked things just the way they were. She wanted to keep working at the library, keep drinking a little wine at night, keep playing triangular chess. She wanted to be outdoors right now, in that glorious sunlight, with the icy air stinging her face. The signs! She wanted to lash out at her mother, tell her that she needn't bother to knit that pair of booties. Her sister-in-law's baby would be born blue with its umbilical cord wrapped tightly around its neck.

Screaming. Sheets soaked with sweat and blood. Lily's mother crouching between splayed legs, her hair fallen out of its habitual knot at the nape of her neck. Urging her daughter-in-law to push, push hard. Lily's poor sister-in-law, screaming and groaning, grunting, grunting a baby out of her womb and onto the counterpane. Still, strangled, lifeless. Her sister-in-law whispering, what is it, a girl or a boy? Lily's mother biting her lower lip. Stifling hot in that room, like this one.

Lily held her tongue and rolled out pie crusts. *Hallie's misfortune. I will make you regret the day you were born.* Keep quiet, count your blessings. You and your notions, you and your notions.

Lily asked her mother what time she was planning to go

over to the Grange for the dance. Early, her mother said. They were only making an appearance, since Lily's father was the Grange secretary. But they wouldn't be staying long; her dancing days were over. Nonsense, Lily said, you're never too old to dance.

Lily's mother stopped crimping pies. She wiped her hands on her apron and caught Lily's gaze. There's a time for kicking up your heels, she said, and a time for stepping back to the sidelines to enjoy watching others do it. You have to recognize when your time has come. Lily flushed and bent to her rolling pin. Her mother wasn't given to this sort of blunt sermonizing now that she was grown. Well, Lily said, she hardly thought it was time for her mother to be staying home to play Parcheesi with the old folks. Besides, she and Ian were going to play the new song they had been working on.

Lily's mother pursed her lips. She picked up two of the completed pies and put them in the oven. She wasn't necessarily talking about herself, she said upon her return to the table. And anyway, it was time for Ian to find himself a wife.

Out in the barnyard, Lily gulped great breaths of fresh air. Why was she constantly doing this? She felt as though she had just been released from school. Oh, she loved her mother—she *did*—but it was always work between the two of them. Lessons to be learned, sewing to be critiqued, chores to be added to the list. Never any of the long, full silences she shared with her father. She missed him, suddenly. It was a longing that cut to her heart. She could see herself crawling into his lap to watch the sun set from his favorite rocker on the porch. She could feel his strong arms around her, his great hands resting in her lap, his chin perched on her collarbone. She could hear their deep silence drenched in cricket songs and the creak of oak against oak—communion.

They both liked it simple, she and her father. And she wondered about this: how simple she liked it, and how complicated, in practice, it actually was.

She should probably go home and darn socks or start supper. But she knew she wouldn't. She had been raised with boys. Could she help it if she liked boy things better?

Eventually she found the twins. They were with the sugaring sledge at the north end of the maple grove. Ian was giving the workhorses their oats while Oren unhooked buckets from taps and emptied them into the tub mounted on the runners of the sledge.

"Did you miss me?" Lily called.

"Those aren't work clothes," Oren shouted back.

He was right. She was wearing a long skirt and one of her faded calico blouses—the uniform of her mother's kitchen. But she had prepared for the possibility that sugaring would not be over by the time she was released from pie-making. Pie-making: a bad taste, like castor oil, on her tongue—one that might be washed away with the overpowering taste of boiling sap. She hiked up her skirt. She was wearing her barn Levis underneath, along with her heavy wool socks and hobnailed boots.

"That's my girl," Oren crowed. "Grab a bucket. We're late back at the sugarhouse. Your brother'll scalp us."

Indians, both of them. Abenaki Indians were the first to make maple syrup—or so the legend went. They taught the first French settlers how to collect sap and boil it. The French gave the Indians religion, the Catholic Church, in return. And small pox.

Lily leaned against the nearest maple and shimmied out of her skirt. She slung it over the seat of the sledge after retrieving a couple of mealy apples from the pockets. She had smuggled these from her mother's kitchen to give to Molly and Dan. The new Dan. All of the Willard Belgians had been named Molly and Dan since before she was born. Farm animals were named like that.

You didn't make pets out of them. When a Dan died, you replaced him with a younger Dan. You never had to think twice when you called to him. But who, she wondered, had named the original Molly and Dan? She plodded over to one of the uncollected trees and lifted the tin lid from the closest bucket. Her prediction earlier that morning had been right: the sap was running beautifully and the bucket was brimming. The aroma that wafted up to her was sweet. It made her want to dip her finger in and suck it. But she didn't bother. She knew she would taste virtually nothing except galvanized steel. It took more than thirty gallons of the stuff to make a single gallon of syrup. The sweetness was in the distilling. She unhooked the bucket from the notched iron spigot and made for the sledge.

The three of them collected sap in silence. Lily's mind cleared, as it always did during hard physical labor. For several minutes she focused on unhooking, trudging over to the tub, emptying, trudging back to the tree and rehanging—thinking about nothing at all. She began to hum a tune, one from her childhood, one that her father used to hum while they were rocking on the front porch. She began to sing the lyrics:

> Monday's child is fair of face
> Tuesday's child is full of grace
> Wednesday's child is in the know
> Thursday's child has far to go

She became keenly aware of the woods around her. Snow from the previous evening's storm had clung to every living surface. Each branch and twig of the glade was coated in white. The sun was at that particular angle, a couple of hours before it would set for the day, where it gilded the edges of everything in gold. It was a sight that she had seen her entire life—forest after a snowstorm— but one that still took her breath away, that made her stop whatever she was doing and wonder for a moment whether there really was a God after all.

She turned to the twins. She found that they had also stopped walking. But they were not staring at the woods, they were staring at her. "What is it?" she said. She could see her breath freezing and sinking until it evaporated again. "What's wrong?" Neither of them answered. "It's beautiful here, isn't it? So quiet."

"You were singing," Oren said.

"So?"

"We haven't heard you sing since we were little boys."

How could this be true? There was music all around them. They were practicing their fiddles all the time. Surely she had hummed this song and dozens like it. But the more she thought about it, the more she realized she didn't sing all that much. Their music together was always without words—tunes rather than songs.

"Don't you know any songs?" she asked.

"Only that one," Oren said. "But we can't remember all the words."

There was so much they had never gotten, so many of the basics that children grew up with: mothers and schooling, nursery rhymes and songs, games and make-believe. It was preposterous, really. They were so ill-prepared for daily life. And yet they suffered little. They were generally happier than anyone else she knew.

She couldn't think of how to respond. So she knelt instead and made a snowball. She chucked it at Ian, and it splattered in the middle of his chest. He looked stunned. They both did. She laughed. Ian grinned, unsure. But then he stooped and made a snowball of his own. Oren followed suit. The game was on. They raced among the maple trees, shrieking and pelting each other with snowballs. Molly and Dan stared with frank curiosity. Eventually the twins ganged up on Lily and sacked her. And as the three of them lay in a heap, gasping for breath, flakes of snow drifted down from the branches above. Lily told them to get off. They didn't move and she didn't insist. She began to sing the nursery rhyme again. This time they sang along, memorizing the words after a couple of rounds.

Time passed.

"Angels," she whispered, finally.

"No, you," Ian said.

"What?"

"You are."

"I meant in the snow. We could make them."

"What are you talking about?" Oren said.

They had never made snow angels, either. Add that to the list. "Get off," Lily said. "I'll show you." She found a stretch of pristine snow and fell backward into it, arms spread wide. She began to flap them as if she were flying. She opened and closed her legs, like a crazy clock. Now it was the twins who were looking on, fascinated. The horses had dropped their heads, sidled up to each other for warmth and dozed off. "Help me up," Lily said to Oren, sitting and holding out her hand. He hoisted her onto her feet and the three of them inspected her handiwork. "See?" she said, pointing at the impression she had made. "A snow angel. Now you try."

They set to work populating the maple grove with a host of angels.

Lily suddenly noticed that the light among the tree trunks had gone very blue, the gloom of a church. The sun had disappeared. They dusted each other off and hurried to finish filling the tub. It was nearly dark by the time the sledge reached Lily's brother's sugarhouse, nestled into the hillside at the opposite end of the grove. Woodsmoke was curling out of the stove pipe, steam was escaping out of the cupola in great billows. Now that the first run was really on, Lily's brother would be boiling night and day until the thaw was over. If you wanted to make any money at it, you bothered with sleep later. They pulled the sledge up the ramp at the back of the sugarhouse to empty the tub into the shack's holding tank. Ian opened the spigot with a wrench and let the sap drain into the tank. It was all done with gravity. Oren gave the horses more oats and covered their backs with blankets. Then the three of them made their way to the front.

"Where have you been?" Lily's brother said when they burst through the door. "I was about to send the dogs after you. Christ you're all wet—all of you. What in hell happened?"

Lily couldn't answer right away, so overwhelmed was she by the sweet hot steam inside. She could barely breathe. The air caught in her nostrils, sticky as candy. It would cling to her clothes and hair long after she left the sugarhouse. When she woke in the morning, she would smell it on her pillow. Oren told him they had lost their way, that every direction looked the same in the heart of the grove. Thank goodness for Lily, he said, who had stumbled upon them and put them back on the right track—their guardian angel.

Her brother snorted and passed around a flask. He told Ian to stoke the stove. Ironwood and ash: the furnace needed to burn white hot. The sap was beginning to thicken in the center compartments of a vast rectangular vat, partitioned like a heaving, roiling maze. He needed to open the spigot from the holding tank and let more sap into the deep end. The difference in heat and density would push the "steamed off" sap into shallower compartments where the water would continue to evaporate out of the distilling sap. He told Lily and Oren to each grab a wooden paddle. They could help him channel the thickening syrup around to the shallowest end where the heat was more intense.

Once Ian had stoked the furnace, he grabbed a baby bottle and began sprinkling cream onto the hot spots he had created. A few drops could calm an entire roiling compartment. They

worked in companionable silence, under the direction of Lily's brother. There could only be one boss in a sugarhouse. You did whatever the master boiler told you. Every second counted now. The exact moment you drained the syrup out of the shallow end into awaiting tins made all the difference between whether the syrup would be fancy-grade, or merely A- or B-grade. You only got fancy from the first run. But you saved everything—even the scorched C-grade for cooking. The dregs you sold off in old milk cans to a molasses dealer who used it in flavoring pipe tobacco. Lily lost track of time, paddling sap from compartment to compartment.

Another sugarhouse at another time. The twins as quarrelsome little boys now. Mr. Pritchard directing the boiling, telling them to hush up and mind what they're doing. Stepping outside to take a piss. Oren ordering Ian to let more sap into the vat. Ian telling him to do it himself. Oren insisting he is in charge because he is the oldest. Ian throwing his paddle down and making for the holding tank's tap. Stopping as he passes his brother, whirling around and grabbing him by the back of the neck, forcing his face into the vat of boiling sap—

"Mind what you're doing!" Oren cried. "You're sloshing syrup over the side."

"Don't take that tone with me, Oren Pritchard!" Lily said.

Oren's face dropped. "I didn't mean anything by it," he said. "I'm sorry, Lil."

Ian saved the moment by breaking into a grin. "Give him hell, Lily," he said. The three of them laughed. They almost never disagreed on anything.

The door flew open. It was Lily's sister-in-law. "Oh," she said to Lily, "I didn't expect to see you here. I thought you were over at the farm baking with your mother."

"I was," Lily said. "But it's all hands on deck when sugaring."

"That's true enough," her sister-in-law agreed. "I've brought food for the menfolk. But there's plenty." She was balancing two stacked baking sheets in one hand and a skillet of raw sausages in the other. She set the skillet on top of the furnace, next to the eternally warming coffee pot. She uncovered the baking sheets to reveal donuts, just raised. One by one she set these in the boiling sap. Next, from her apron pockets, she produced nearly a dozen eggs. She cracked these open on the side of the vat and poached them alongside the donuts. When the sausages were sizzling in the skillet, she asked Lily to fetch plates from the shelf. She took a slotted spoon from its hook in the rafters and scooped out first the caramelized eggs, then the donuts, placing a couple of each on a plate along with several links of sausage. "Supper!" she called over to her husband. They all ate in silence, sopping up the yolk with bites of donut. The way of farmfolk when there's a job to do. It was all unspeakably sweet, of course, but they ate every last scrap of food, sucking on sour pickles afterward. Lily wondered if she could possibly be happier.

Mercifully, Hallie did not turn up at the Sugar-On-Snow Dance. Lily still hadn't come to terms with Hallie's violent outburst at the library. And the gossip about her husband was growing vicious. More to *that* story than met the eye, everyone was saying. The woman who cleaned house for Hallie knew for a fact that she and her husband had always slept in separate bedrooms. According to the bank secretary, that handsome young teller from Marshfield—the one who was prettier than some of the girls— had suddenly given his notice about a week after Hallie's husband. It was widely known that Hallie's husband, once he had had a few beers at hunting camp, would throw his arms around his buddies and kiss them good-night. Nobody had thought anything of it at the time. *You know the way men are when they've been drinking.*

One of the boys in the band offered Lily the jug. She took a pull off it. The sinus-clearing rush of home-brew. She winced. These days, every farmer was making his own corn liquor, whether he had any talent for it or not. She took another sip. She needed to calm her nerves or she would never be able to play. The new song. A few minutes later, she took another. And then another. She didn't eat nearly enough at the buffet table to compensate. After all that pie-making, she couldn't bear the thought of food. And she had never liked the sugar-on-snow candy the old ladies made by pouring hot boiling syrup onto trays of snow and then picking out the squiggly bits of taffy with a fork. It made your back teeth stick together. So by the time the Grange Hall was full, she was well on her way to being tipsy. The band began their square dances in earnest. She wasn't playing properly at all—not that it really mattered. Ian was the real draw. She was only backing him up. Second fiddle. Besides, everyone was there to have a good time. If it had a beat, they would dance to it. If it had a tune, they would sing along. And the more the crowd stomped and clapped, the better the band played. The more they played, the thirstier they got. Another pull off the jug.

Every once in a while, Oren would lure Lily off the stage to dance with him. They would spin around the room together, laughing at how mismatched they were in height. Judging by the flush in Oren's cheeks, he was nipping at the corn liquor himself. He told Lily that he didn't know what had gotten into him—he hated big social events—but he was having a good time at this one. He had taken it upon himself to ask every spinster and widow in Cabot Fields for a jig. He had even charmed Lily's mother into a reel. Lily tried to make eye contact with her mother. When she did, she was surprised by how stony-faced and disapproving the return gaze was. Had her mother caught her nipping at the jug? A few moments later, her mother donned her coat and dragged her father, stumbling, out the door by the sleeve of his coat. Lily wouldn't let herself read anything into this. Her mother had already warned her they would only be staying an hour or two.

Lily's duet with Ian went well. They played it while the other members of the band were taking a break. Everyone stopped to listen. The applause was more than just polite. The men clapped Ian on the back, the women hugged Lily and told her they were proud. Flushed, Lily accepted their praise and a glass of punch.

She had always thought of herself as a shy girl. Yet she had never felt more powerful than when she was performing. Her heart opened up and her true self came tumbling out. Her true self knew she was different from everyone else and knew that her differences made her beautiful—if unconventional. Her true self wasn't shy about her differences, but celebrated them. Her true self liked the attention.

It was her true self, then, who waltzed with both of the twins at the same time.

Later she would say that she had been spurred on by the music, by the heat of the moment, by one too many pulls off the jug. But it hadn't really happened like that. It hadn't been some sort of dare or cut-up or way of shocking her neighbors. Truth was, she hadn't given it a single thought—not until it was too late. Ian had simply asked her to dance when the band struck back up. It wasn't one of the tunes that needed his fiddling to carry the melody. Accepting a dance with your brother-in-law was the most natural thing in the world. He looked so much like her husband that probably no one would even have noticed. But then Oren himself stepped up behind her and kissed her neck. He reached around her back and placed his hands over hers. He followed her, following Ian's lead. This was the only unusual part of it, really: it was Ian who most often followed Oren. The three of them circled the dance floor. They laughed each time they stumbled over one another; but they quickly found the tempo again and carried on.

They were enjoying themselves so much that the music seemed to stop before the song was finished. Lily whirled around to clap for more.

They were the only ones dancing. Everyone else was watching them, including the band. And no one else in the Grange Hall was laughing.

Two weeks later, Lily received a letter from the Cabot Fields Board of Selectmen. The board would no longer be needing her services as librarian. It seemed that the library's hours of operation had been erratic at best for the better part of two years. Employees of the town were required to conduct themselves with the highest degree of professionalism, given that they served in many ways as role models for the town's youth and citizenry at large. Lily should remand her keys to the Town Clerk's office at her earliest convenience. The Board of Selectmen wished her the very best in her future endeavors.

"But no one cares that the library was closed for a couple of extra hours in the afternoon," she sobbed to Oren. "And anyway, it's been months since that happened. Why didn't they say something to me sooner? Of course I would have kept it open."

"This isn't about that," Oren said.

"Well what do I do?"

"Nothing. Stay home and plant a garden as soon as the snow melts," he said, hugging her close. "Take care of your horses. It wasn't much of a salary, anyway. We'll get by well enough on what the carpentry business brings in."

Lily did some long-overdue cleaning that spring. She practiced her fiddle, caught up on her reading, planted a kitchen garden. Oren and Ian came home for lunch every day. Partly this was to keep her company. Partly it was to begin work on a horse barn. Oren kept the design simple—to be sure of getting a roof over the horses' heads by fall—though the barn would be big enough to accommodate six stalls. There could be a new colt or two by the next spring.

One morning, Lily was out hoeing the radishes when she unearthed a curious object. It was a soapstone, the size of a silver dollar, almost perfectly round with a hole bored into its center. Emanating from the hole were concentric grooves and between each of these were minutely carved figures and hatches—a language she did not speak. Indian money, she guessed, used by one of the local tribes to keep track of trade. But the longer she fingered the rings and contemplated the messages, the more certain she grew that the stone was from a culture far older. What if, once upon a time, the grooves themselves contained information, one piece of information per groove, one idea per day. What if wisdom had been stored there, wisdom that had been learned and lost and re-learned and lost again. She ran her thumbnail around the outside groove. Monday's child is fair of face, she whispered, substituting words she knew—for now. Monday's lesson. She tucked the soapstone into her apron pocket and bent back to her task.

Her thoughts drifted to all the forgotten books in her little library, the tomes she had faithfully dusted once a week because no one ever checked them out. They too contained whole alphabets of idea, thoughts that had once been considered important enough to decipher. Truths changed and got replaced. And what about all the truths that weren't even in the library, in books she had not been allowed to purchase from the traveling booksellers? Cabot Fields had fairly narrow taste when it came to truth. Mathematics, horse husbandry, quilting, Protestant religions and trout fishing. Cowboy serials were the most popular novels in her library, then Gothic thrillers. Effusive Victorian romances were frowned upon—unless they were considered Classics. These were begrudgingly allowed, along with Greek tragedies and a few French novels, if there was a possibility they would be required reading at school. She grimaced. *Her library.*

Here in her vegetable patch, she could rationalize her dismissal from the library as the work of a few mean-spirited men. It was easy enough to soothe her hurt pride with self-righteousness. But this small comfort evaporated the moment she left her property. In Cabot Fields, she felt the town's disapproval keenly. Censure was palpable in every hello she exchanged on the street, every purchase she made, every errand she ran.

She stood and scanned the horizon for rain clouds. She surveyed her morning's work. She sighed. Time to run a few of those errands now. With heavy feet, she stored her hoe in the toolshed, washed her hands and face at the kitchen sink, donned her straw bonnet. She didn't have to make these pilgrimages down the Peacham Farm Road, she supposed. The twins could bring whatever was needed on their way home from work. But to hide or to show fear was as good as admitting guilt. At first, Oren had chided her for imagining any such judgment or disapproval—until the next Grange dance. Suddenly, two of the band members came down with the flu. Too few townsfolk turned out to form proper square dance sets. The dance ended two hours early.

Lily's first stop was the General Store. She needed a few groceries for dinner—Oren had left her a list. Each aisle she entered was curiously empty, though she could hear the chatter of familiar voices all around her. Each gathering of neighbors she approached was just finishing a conversation and disbanding. None of them was rude. They all smiled, nodded hello, asked about her folks. But all of them apologized for being in a hurry and pressed on. No inquiries about her own health, no chitchat about the weather, no town gossip.

At the meat counter, Lily asked the butcher for a roasting chicken. He claimed to have sold the last one ten minutes earlier. She told him a turkey would do. There hadn't been any of those in a week. How about a few lean pork chops, then? He suggested she try the butcher over in Danville. Mondays were tough around here. Lily squinted at her grocery list to hold the tears back. She would take the sausages, she said—those that were right there in the front of the case.

She slammed out of the store, clutching her basket in both arms. How dare they judge her! It was just a tipsy turn around the dance floor! She stalked off in the direction of the bank, keeping her head down, avoiding anyone else's gaze. She didn't notice Hallie until it was too late.

Lily recognized her shoes—prim patent leather with fashionable new laces. Their eyes met when she looked up. Hallie's expression surprised her—not anger or smugness but bemusement, as though she were finally seeing something obvious that had been right under her nose the whole time. Neither of them spoke, but Hallie offered her a faint smile. Lily smiled back, uncertainly, before taking the steps of the bank two at a time.

By harvest, they knew something had to be done. Oren delivered the news at supper: Reverend Higgins would not need the twins to build the new steeple after all. Though the Elders were very happy with the ceiling—not to mention the fine new pews—they had learned of the Pritchards' Indian heritage and felt that it might be inappropriate for them to be working in a house of God. The Elders had decided instead to contract a firm out of Marshfield. Lily lost her appetite for the food on her plate. "But they can't do that," she said. "They already promised you the job. You could take them to court."

"We haven't got anything in writing," Oren said. "We've never worked that way. We'll just have to find another job to replace it."

"It won't be around here," Ian said. "Unless something changes pretty damn quick, we're going to have to take the corn van on the road again."

All three pushed the food on their plates around in silence.

"I'm not going to be driven from my home over one silly little dance!" Lily exclaimed, slamming her fork down on the table. "They're not even giving us a chance to put things right. What do they want? A public flogging?"

"Go ask your mother what to do," Ian said, quietly. "She'll know."

"Don't be ridiculous," Oren said.

Her mother: a quiet woman who had never once stuck out. Not a rare beauty, not a terrible gossip, not renowned baker, not a fashionable dresser, not the chair of a single church committee. A woman defined more by what she wasn't than what she was.

"No, he's right," Lily said, after a moment. "She'll know."

Lily didn't sleep well that night. She had barely spoken with her parents since the trouble began. Apart from farm business and sending the occasional basket of produce back and forth, they had pretty much kept to themselves. But Lily remembered the conversation she had had with her mother at pie-making. Her mother rarely ventured opinions unsolicited. But if asked, Lily knew, she would have plenty to say on the subject of her behavior. Lily tossed and turned, imagining what this would be. At first light, she was still awake. She got up, got dressed, crossed the Peacham Farm Road, and went straight to her mother's kitchen.

Of course her mother was already up. Lily joined her at the cookstove, where she was frying bacon. "Pour yourself a cup of coffee," her mother said. "I've just made some fresh." Lily helped herself and sat at the kitchen table. It was all so familiar: the dried herbs above the stove, the white chintz curtains, the gleaming linoleum on the floor, the old wind-up clock ticking away on the wall, her mother frying bacon.

"We didn't mean anything by it," Lily said, after a moment.

"Ain't none of my business," her mother said.

"Then how come everybody's making it their business?"

Lily's mother turned, her fork dripping grease onto the linoleum. "You were the one who made it everybody's business, young lady."

"It was just a little dance," Lily said. "It's the twentieth century, for Pete's sake. Women have the vote now."

"You know better than that," Lily's mother said. She pointed behind her, to The Knoll, her fork glinting in the lamplight. "What the three of you get up to on that hill is your own business. You can be as modern as you like—only God can be your judge about that. But what it *looks* like you're getting up to, that's everyone's business. And you can bet your life the town'll be happy to sit in judgment."

Lily began to cry. Her mother took the skillet off the fire and wiped her hands on her apron. She refilled her own coffee cup and sat in the chair across from Lily. "Well, what do I do now?" Lily snuffled.

Her mother took a thoughtful sip of coffee. "If you don't want them to be thinking something," she said, "you've got to show them what else to think."

Clock ticking.

"And what exactly do you and Daddy think?"

"I already told you it ain't none of my business," she said.

Lily was miserable. Miserable, because she knew her mother was right. She had lived in Cabot Fields all her life. She knew what the rules were. There weren't many of them, but they were clear. She stood to go. Then she sat back down. She swallowed her pride.

She asked her mother for help. Her mother patted her hand. She would see what she could do, she said. The ladies were having a quilting bee later that afternoon. They would be raffling the quilt off at the Grange's Christmas bazaar. Lily stood again. Her mother urged her to stay for breakfast, there was plenty No, Lily said, it was time to be getting back. She had bacon to fry of her own.

She crossed paths with her father in the barnyard. He was just coming off the morning milking. He asked her what had brought her across the road so early. She told him she had had a good long talk with her mother. You get everything straightened out? he asked, taking her hand and squeezing it. Lily nodded. Good girl, he said. That's good. He wanted to know when they were all coming over for supper. He hadn't seen them in a while, hadn't had a good game of chess since, well, he couldn't remember when. Lily hugged her father—she knew then that she had been forgiven—and promised to bring a pot of baked beans before the week was out. That's good, he said. You do that. Lily wiped her eyes and told him she had best be getting on. He assured her she would be all right. The Willards were tougher than boiled owls, he said.

The next night there was an unexpected knock at the door. The three of them were sitting in the parlor, gathered around the hearth. The first cold evening of the year, a real bite of autumn in the air. Oren and Ian were carving chess pieces, Lily was practicing her fiddle. They glanced up at each other when they heard the three sharp raps. Ian went to get the door. A moment later, he returned with Hallie.

Goodness, she said, had it ever gotten chilly outside. Lily and Oren murmured their hellos. Lily invited Hallie to sit, offering her a glass of wine. Hallie declined. She perched at the edge of Lily's sofa and began warming her hands at the fire. She could only stay a moment, she said. She had run into Lily's mother at the quilting bee the afternoon before. They had had such a nice visit. It had made Hallie realize she hadn't seen Lily in ages and ages.

Yes, Lily said. That's true. Lily wondered how long it would take Hallie to get to the point. She wasn't entirely sure how to pry it out of her, either. Not knowing what else to do, she picked up her fiddle and began playing again. My, wasn't this cozy? Hallie said before long. It made such a nice change from her big old empty house. Lily stopped playing. Hallie was always welcome, she said. She could come by anytime.

Hallie smiled and settled back on the sofa. They all knew, didn't they, that her marriage was over? The annulment had gone through swiftly, given the particularity of the circumstances. Well, what was done, was done. High time to forget the whole mess and get on with it. She, for one, would be happy when life got back to normal around Cabot Fields.

They all nodded.

"Which one of you is Ian?" Hallie said. "I swear I don't know how you tell them apart, Lily."

Lily looked over at the twins. It was true, they were virtually identical again. In the past year, Ian had gained back almost all of the weight he had lost. They were both brown from working outside in the sun. They wore the same clothes, out of the same closet. Once a month, Lily gave them the same haircut with her sewing scissors. Yet, somehow, Lily knew them on sight now. She no longer needed to glance at their wrists to see whether it was a white or black bracelet. She had learned the minute differences of their personalities and how these were expressed in their features, in their movements. Oren looked older to her by ten years, not thirteen minutes. He was more responsible, protective, bookish, bossy. Ian seemed bigger physically. Bigger than life—a war hero—

dashing from all his adventures. Quicker with a joke. Flirtatious, carefree, creative.

But, she supposed, for anyone else to tell them apart, they would have to know about the bracelets. Or the scars.

"I'm Ian," Ian said.

Or the bullet holes.

"Why the last time I saw you was at Lily's wedding. You didn't weigh more than a hundred pounds soaking wet. I'm glad to see you got your voice back. Now Ian, I was wondering if I could prevail upon you to walk me home. I'm fine when it's light outside. But I get a little nervous after dark. You hear stories about wolves lurking along the roadside."

Ian glanced over at his brother, then at Lily. Hallie had clearly had no trouble walking over in the dark. Lily looked down at the fiddle in her lap. She understood now. She understood the purpose of Hallie's visit. Her mother had seen to it. She understood what new thing she needed to give the town to think. Oh, the ingenuity of women! She hated them. And she hated herself for what she was about to do.

She cleared her throat. "I think that's a fine idea," she said. She forced herself to look up and smile at the twins, then at Hallie. "Though I insist, Hallie, that you come over for a proper visit tomorrow night. I'll make something nice for supper. And then maybe we can convince you to stay for a game of cards afterward." She looked at Oren again. She held his gaze until he understood that it was his line.

"We won't accept no for an answer," Oren said. "Will we, Ian?"

"Yes," Ian said. "I mean no. I'll just get my coat."

That Ian's delivery was as unconvincing as his brother's seemed to matter little to Hallie. She stood, beaming. "I'll only accept for Ian's sake," she said. "I know how tiresome it can be to feel like the fifth wheel."

"Then it's settled," Lily said, standing as well.

"What time will you have me?" Hallie asked, making for the hallway.

"Scven," Lily said. "Ian will pick you up in the truck just before seven."

5

✳

LOVING AND GIVING

[1 9 2 2 – 1 9 2 3]

LILY HADN'T STEPPED FOOT INSIDE the First Congregational Church of Cabot Fields since her own wedding, two and a half years earlier. Yet something about the smell of it—dust mixed with candle wax, moldy hymnal pages, the cloying scent of Easter lilies—gave her a dizzying sense of repeating time. She felt as though she were suffocating in this robin's-egg blue dress. Sweat stung her eyes beneath the matching tulle veil. It was one of the hottest Mays anyone could remember. She worried she would faint before the long-winded Reverend Higgins pronounced Ian and Hallie man and wife.

Tying the knot. Lily thought of the rope swing at the swimming hole, the one dangling from the old swamp willow. She hadn't been swimming in ages, probably not since she and Oren had taken Ian there upon his return from the war. The swing had several big knots tied to the end of it. You stood on whichever one you dared in order to swing out over the pool—the higher up the rope, the more dangerous the dive. A fiddle string. You tied a knot in the bottom end and threaded the rest through the base plate. You stretched the string over the bridge, threading it through a tuning peg at the fiddle's neck, cranking the peg until it was taut. You kept cranking and stretching until the string sang at the right pitch. It had been so long since she and Ian had played together. For months now, he had spent most of his evenings with Hallie, escorting her to the Opera House in Danville, taking her for long horse rides on Saturday afternoon. A hangman's rope.

She had advocated their courtship every step of the way. She and Oren had attended the Grange's Christmas Bazaar with Ian and Hallie. They had gone to her parents' New Year's Eve gathering as a foursome. Same with the children's Easter egg hunt on the town common. Lunch after lunch in Hallie's kitchen, planning first the morning ceremony then the breakfast afterward. Hour after hour in Hallie's sewing room, making her gown. Hallie insisting on white in spite of it all, finally compromising on cream-colored satin. A brand new dress. Hours in Hallie's fussy little parlor, tatting her floor-length veil. Hallie waxing romantic about the honeymoon they would take to Montreal, the number of children they would have, what their names would be, what Ian would eventually make of himself with Hallie at his side to guide him, what good times she and Lily would share as sisters. And after all these months of hours, here Lily was, finally, standing in the stifling heat of this horrible church, clutching at the very veil she had helped Hallie to make, making sure her oldest friend didn't trip on it or snag it on a floor nail.

Repeating time. The very same morning wedding as her own, two and a half years earlier. Fitted satin dress with a long lace veil, church ceremony attended by most of the town, wedding breakfast at the mother of the bride's. Restrained, stiff, formal. Lily's wedding was Hallie's too—planned by her and based on her first one to the banker. They were all Hallie's weddings, really.

Lily gripped the bouquet Hallie had ordered for her and squeezed her eyes shut. But she couldn't seem to read this moment for signs, or wander away from it to peek into rooms of the future. She was, for some odd reason, stuck right here, in the here and now—not knowing—while Reverend Higgins droned on and on about having and holding from this day forward, honoring and cherishing, for better or worse, for richer or poorer, in sickness and in health, till death parted them. Not knowing what life would be like once the knot was tied.

Finally it was. Finally Ian's ring was slipped onto Hallie's finger. Finally the organ struck up "The Wedding March." Finally they processed down the aisle, Lily still clutching at Hallie's train, desperate for a breath of fresh air.

Oren sidled up to her at the reception. She was sitting alone on a swing under an old maple in the backyard, minding the children while the grown-ups danced, rocking and fanning herself with a handkerchief. Ian and the band were inside playing, she could hear strains of "The Gentlemen's Waltz." Hallie had counseled Lily not to bring her own fiddle; it would seem unladylike for the matron of honor to be sawing away in a satin dress. Oren bent to kiss her forehead. She could smell Canadian Club on his breath. "Sit for minute," she said, patting the seat next to her. "And give me a sip of whatever is sloshing around in your coat pocket." He slumped into the swing and handed her a flask. She unscrewed the cap and took a long gulp.

"Easy, there!" Oren grinned. "I don't want to have to carry you home over my shoulder."

"I wish you would," Lily said, handing back the flask.

They sat for a moment, husband and wife. He was a good man. Strong as her father, but far gentler. Hardworking, but also enormously talented with his hands. Handsome as anything she had ever seen. Sometimes she worried that he had come to her too easily. After all, he had practically declared his intention to marry her when he was nine years old. A decade later he had turned up to claim her. She had never really allowed herself to be

courted by anyone else because she had been waiting for him—
she knew that now. And yet their marriage wasn't so easy, not
really. Because they weren't each other's everything. There was always the matter of Ian. They both knew what Oren was like without his twin. He was diminished in some way, less of himself. This
is what was on both of their minds as they rocked: losing Ian. Ian's
marriage to Hallie could not be compared to him going off to
war—he would be back after his honeymoon—but today was the
first day they would begin living with their loss.

Oren took her hand. His was so much larger than her own,
callused and scarred, broken-nailed, brown as boot leather. He
traced the delicate veins of her wrist with fingertips rough as
sandpaper. Long, thick fingers with chipped pink nails. It tickled
and Lily giggled. He raised her hand to his lips and kissed her
knuckles, nibbling on them. She flushed suddenly, whiskey and
desire warming in her belly. He lowered their hands to his lap.
She could feel him stirring in his good suit, feel the hard sinews of
his upper thigh. She leaned into him and they rocked like that for
a moment, while she fondled him under the cover of his big hand.

"Let's get out of here," he said.

"It's too early for us to begin making our good-byes," she
said. "Everyone will take it as a signal that the party's over."

"Then let's just leave."

"Oren, don't be ridiculous—" But he kissed her, stifling her
objections. She felt his tongue parting her lips and poking at her
teeth. She opened her mouth. Whiskey, as well as the more familiar tastes of him: mown hay and licorice, green apples, honey. "I'll
go grab my gloves from the hall table," she said. "I'll meet you
round front."

They made love that entire afternoon and into the night. It
was different from any time before. No beginning or middle or
end. They stopped to talk, doze, eat. And they did it to each

other—this was new. At certain moments it was Oren taking her while she gripped his scarred buttocks, Oren straining to meld into her, trying to take up residency in her body so that he wouldn't feel so desperately alone. But at other moments, it was definitely her taking him, filling the void left behind, filling it with her tongue, her fingers, her sex. It was while Lily was taking him that she felt—for the very first time, perhaps for the last—as though *she* were Oren's twin, not Ian.

Sometime after midnight she left him among the tangled damp sheets, sleeping. Her mind was too full of new thoughts. She wandered through her house naked, locking doors, closing curtains, straightening furniture, fluffing pillows; feeling the different delicious textures beneath her feet of rag rug and polished wood, cool slate and rough brick. Eventually, she found herself in the doorway of Ian's and Hallie's new room. The twins had closed in a screen porch on the opposite side of the house. They had filled it with Hallie's frilly bedroom furniture, to make her feel at home.

Ian had drawn the line at moving into Hallie's house in town. She had threatened to call the engagement off, but he had remained firm. A couple of weeks had passed and then Hallie had put her house up for sale. Ian would simply not live in a place her ex-husband had bought and paid for, Hallie had confided to her church sewing circle. He would only live in a house he had built himself. Before long, the entire town had heard the story; and their estimation of Ian's character had risen. It was the price you had to pay to marry a strong-willed man, most had agreed. It was now widely speculated that Lily and Oren would sell them a piece of land, that the boys would begin building another house as soon as Hallie was expecting.

Lily wondered about this, and many other things. She closed the door. The room hadn't shown her anything of what life would be like once the newlyweds had returned from Montreal.

She got herself a glass of water from the kitchen and made her way back to Oren. Sometimes she understood Ian—especially when they were playing together or minding the horses—but sometimes he felt like a complete stranger. So she would have to wait and see, just like everyone else. This, she knew, would not stop her from lying awake most of the night, worrying.

Hallie banished all the cats to the horse barn just after Independence Day. One of them had jumped up onto the table to lick the butter. Cats were not pets, she maintained; they earned their keep micing. This was also the last night they ate supper in the kitchen. What was the point in having a nice big dining room, Hallie chided, if they didn't use it? She also insisted they call their evening meal dinner, not supper—she thought it more civilized. Dinner was not the midday meal, that was lunch. They didn't have to talk like farmers just because they lived in a farm community. Oren had already been relieved of any cooking responsibility upon their return from Montreal. Hallie thought it scandalous that a man would be expected to do both the cooking and the bread-winning. Unfortunately, she did not think it appropriate, as Oren's replacement, that they should all chat around the kitchen table while she chopped and mixed and fried. It was at dinner, and not before, that they should engage in what she called the art of conversation. All board games were, of course, banned until coffee. Coffee was now taken in the parlor. And if the United States Congress saw fit to ban wine-drinking at dinner—or at any other time, for that matter—well, Hallie certainly didn't hold herself above the law, nor should any of the rest of them. All remaining wine bottles were removed to the cellar.

Lily found the art of conversation excruciating—like tea parties with dolls. Before Hallie, in the kitchen, they had never lacked for things to talk about. The twins had matched Lily's anecdotes about the cranky old-timers in the library with their own about the bizarre things they built to make their clients' houses "home." At the very least, they had always brought the town gossip back to The Knoll, like the evening paper. But Hallie declared these topics too common. She preferred to talk about the show she had recently dragged Ian to see at the Opera House, the book she was currently reading, or a disaster that had suddenly befallen someone in town (reversals of fortune weren't gossip) and how it might have been avoided if those concerned had only . . . Lily tried her best to seem interested. Oren ate in utter silence, though he always cleaned his plate. There was no denying that Hallie was a good cook. Ian gazed upon Hallie in silence with what looked to be a mixture of pride at her sophistication and fear that he might be called upon to answer a question. Mercifully, her questions were mostly rhetorical. The art of conversation, where Hallie was concerned, most often turned into a monologue.

Coffee in the parlor tended to be a little less stressful. Hallie allowed them their game of triangular chess—she wasn't much for board games, herself preferring to crochet doilies or embroider pillowcases with her new initials: H B P. It was during one of these games, when Lily was on the verge of puzzling out the moves she would need to checkmate Oren, that Hallie cleared her throat to speak. "I was in town this afternoon," she said, holding her half-finished doily up to the lamp to inspect it for flaws. It looked to Lily like a gigantic tattered spider web. "And who should I run into but Reverend Higgins. We got to talking and he told me that the rectory's library could really use another set of bookshelves. He said he would like nothing better than to hire the Pritchard brothers for the job—you do such fine work, he said—"

"I thought the good Reverend didn't hire heathens," Oren said.

"That was all a big misunderstanding," Hallie said. "His only real concern, he said, was the cost of you both and how to justify it to the Elders."

"You get what you pay for," Oren said. Lily could tell by his tone that he didn't like where Hallie was headed.

"That's exactly what I said to the Reverend," Hallie exclaimed. "I said, surely something could be worked out whereby the rectory could have Pritchard bookshelves and keep the cost down. Then it struck me like a lightning bolt: Ian could do them all by himself—when the two of you were slow—and charge a little less."

"I hope you didn't suggest that to him," Oren said.

"Why, of course I did," Hallie said, "and he thought it a splendid compromise. He's not in any hurry, and—"

"But we work together," Ian whispered. "We're a team."

"But don't you see? If you're working at one job while Oren is working at another, the two of you could practically double your income."

"And what other job am I supposed to be working at?" Oren asked.

"Well, I don't know, you'd have to find one," Hallie said. "Look how easy it was for me to line this one up."

"Nobody asked you to line anything up, Hallie," Oren said.

"Really, Oren, I resent your tone. I was just trying to help. In any case, it's practically all settled now. I told Reverend Higgins I would send Ian round to the rectory first thing in the morning." Oren stood abruptly, toppling some of the chess pieces. His chair squealed against the floorboards and he stalked out of the room. In the ensuing silence, Ian glanced at Lily, panicked. Lily stared down into her lap. She was too stunned herself to offer much consolation. "Lily," Hallie said, "surely you can see the sense in—"

"Excuse me," Lily said. She fled the parlor in the same direction as her husband. She found Oren seated on the edge of the bed. He had already taken off his shirt, which lay crumpled on the floor. Lily could tell by the way he was tugging at a sock that he was furious. She couldn't remember the last time she had seen him angry—if ever. This frightened her a little. "Can I hole up in here with you," she asked, "or do you need to be alone?" She waited while he freed his foot from the sock and flung it across the room. She watched him wiggle his toes and sigh. Beautiful feet. He looked up and smiled, patted the coverlet beside him, an invitation to sit. When she did, he put his arm around her. A moment later, he lay his head on her shoulder.

"I hate her," he said. "I always have."

"Hush," Lily said. "She means well."

"I know. But I can't for the life of me see what Ian sees in her." He pulled Lily backward so that she was lying in his arms. They both stared up at the ceiling.

"She talks enough for the both of them," Lily ventured.

They both smiled.

"The worst of it is, she's right," Oren said. " If half of our job bids come through, we'll *need* to run two crews. As it is, we'll probably hire your two younger brothers for the rest of the summer. I just can't stand Hallie's meddling. The carpentry business is between me and my brother."

Lily could tell by the steady rise and fall of his chest that he was no longer angry. She held him tight—because she understood his resentment. It was a complicated thing. Since Ian's marriage to Hallie, Pritchard Brothers had gotten a lot busier. They now got bids for new jobs nearly every week, and not just from townsfolk. Requests were coming in from Marshfield and Plainfield, all over the county. It couldn't just be a coincidence. Hallie was good for their business. Curious. Success didn't seem to be making the three of them any happier.

Ian paid a visit to Reverend Higgins the next day. It turned out he didn't really need much in the way of shelves—his library at the rectory was a tiny little room off the kitchen. Ian could

easily build them in an afternoon or two, though at a price that
was half Pritchard Brothers' normal rate. Hallie declared there
had been no harm done after all. Oren nonetheless refused to sit
at the dinner table that night, or the following night. He made
cold sandwiches for himself in the caravan after work. When he
got home, he went straight to his room. On the third night, Hallie finally gave in and apologized for meddling. Only then did
Oren bury the hatchet.

After that, life at The Knoll returned more or less to normal.
Normal, except that the art of conversation at dinner dwindled to
thank-yous for second helpings and requests to pass the butter.
And the games of triangular chess came to an end. Oren retired to
their room immediately after dinner. Ian and Lily played their fiddles for an hour or so, just to keep in practice, but then Lily would
join Oren, leaving Hallie and Ian to their own devices. Lily would
find him on the bed with a pillow propped behind his back, scrib-
bling in a small leather-bound book, practicing his handwriting or
updating his accounts.

The pattern of their lives was interrupted only once that fall.
Lily woke to a noise in the middle of the night. It was very dark in
the room, but she could sense someone else was there. She listened while her eyes adjusted to the shadows. It was Ian, standing
naked at the foot of their bed. "Ian," she whispered. "What is it?
What's wrong?" He didn't respond. He was sound asleep, of
course. Sleepwalking. She debated whether or not to wake him—
or Oren. But before she could decide, Ian turned and left the
room. She listened as he made his way down the stairs, through
the kitchen and back to his own bedroom. His and Hallie's.

One night in November, Hallie slammed her fork down on
the table. They all jumped. "What's wrong?" Lily asked, alarmed.

"I'm so bored!" Hallie cried. "Aren't you bored? My God, we never see anyone else except each other."

"I see people all day long," Oren said mildly. "Too many, if you ask me."

"What about you, Lily? Wouldn't you like a little company?"

Lily shrugged. She had no one to miss, really. Apart from Hallie, she had never cultivated friends. She had always preferred the company of her family. The glistening soap bubble of her circumscribed existence. She frowned. Sometimes, though, she did feel a longing for the past—for the way things were when she was a little girl.

"I know!" Hallie said. "We'll throw a tree-trimming party. We'll invite all our friends from town. Virtually no one has ever been out to The Knoll. It'll give us a chance to show the place off properly." No response. "Well?" Hallie prompted.

"We don't celebrate Christmas much," Oren said.

"Why on earth *would* a couple of bachelors?" Hallie laughed. "But we're a family now. Families celebrate holidays." She lay her hand over Ian's and squeezed it. "Isn't that right, darling?"

Lily expected Ian to glance over at Oren to telegraph his confusion, receive instructions for how to proceed. But he didn't. He smiled weakly at Hallie and nodded.

"There now, it's all settled," Hallie said, pulling her hand away and retrieving the fork from her plate. "For dessert I made pan dowdy from the windfalls in your mother's orchard, Lily— those that weren't too wormy."

But it wasn't all settled, not, at least, in Lily's mind. She waited until after the pan dowdy to voice her concerns, when she and Hallie were alone in the kitchen doing the dishes. "I'm not so sure having a party here is such a good idea," she began.

"Nonsense."

"But what if no one comes? Remember the last Grange dance—"

"That's all buried and forgotten."

"Buried maybe—"

Hallie whirled to face her, her hands dripping with soap suds. "I said, they'll come. They're all curious to know what goes on up here. And we're going to show them. They're going to have a perfectly nice time, and then they're all going to go home a little disappointed."

"What is that supposed to mean?"

"There's nothing less interesting than the ordinary."

Lily resumed wiping plates.

And so the invitations went out: A tree-trimming party at The Knoll, to take place the Saturday afternoon before Christmas. Adults only, please. All refreshments provided. Guests kindly requested to contribute one ornament per couple. RSVP regrets only.

Not a single regret was sent.

Lily and Hallie spent the morning of the party cooking and cleaning. The twins were sent off to the woodlot to find a blue spruce for the parlor. Not a Scotch pine, according to Hallie; not a balsam, not a fir. A spruce—or don't come back at all. They were also given strict guidelines for the tree's size, shape and bushiness. Oren suggested that Lily come along to help pick it out. She at least had an inkling of what a Christmas tree *looked* like. Hallie vetoed the idea. Lily was needed in the kitchen. Cutting the tree was men's work.

The twins returned home with a magnificent spruce. Its topmost branch brushed the ceiling plaster of the parlor's bay window. Hallie instructed Ian to follow her to the attic. The two of them returned with several large cardboard cartons. Some of these contained sprigs of rosemary and sage, dried whole and preserved in cedar shavings. Under Hallie's supervision, Lily and the twins hung them like icicles from the branches. Other boxes contained dried oranges stuck full of cloves, pine cones stuffed with lavender seeds, and cinnamon sticks bundled together with red ribbon. These were pierced with a large sewing needle and hung from the branches on loops of red thread. Once the boxes were emptied, they all stepped back to admire their work. The tree had begun to warm in the room and, in the process, exude an intoxicating scent.

"What a clever girl you are!" Lily said to Hallie.

Hallie offered a wry smile. "You're just realizing that now?"

The first guests arrived promptly at three. There was no pretense of being fashionably late in the country; not when you had chores the following morning at dawn. Hallie, radiant in a new green dress, greeted them in the front foyer and took their coats. As guests continued to pull up in their carriages and automobiles, she dispatched them to the parlor where Lily was stationed to offer them eggnog or punch, and encourage them to hang their ornaments on the tree. Oren carved ham and turkey for sandwiches at a buffet set up in the dining room; Ian circulated among the two rooms, quietly playing what Christmas carols he knew on his fiddle. The parlor was full of laughing, chatting townsfolk. Soon the tree was resplendent with spun glass orbs, punched-tin angels, brass horns, candy canes, gingerbread men, and tiny straw baskets filled with holly berries and mistletoe. Lily's family had come—her parents, her brothers and their wives—as well as Reverend Higgins, the Board of Selectmen, and the new bank president.

Lily eventually escaped to the kitchen, on the pretense of replenishing the buffet, where she was able to unclench her mouth from its forced smile. Along the way, she accepted half a dozen compliments on what a nice party it was. Was it? Mercifully, the kitchen was empty. She thought briefly of stepping out onto the back porch to see if the menfolk were passing around a jug. She thought better of it, remembering the last time. Instead, she tucked a limp curl behind her ear and made for the cold pantry to fetch

another loaf of bread. She stopped short, though, when she realized a couple was occupying the unlit room. She could tell by
their silhouettes that they were standing close with their heads
drawn together, engaged in either a clandestine embrace or dis-
creet disagreement. She listened to the low murmur of a man's
voice. She tried to make sense of his whispered words, though she
knew it was wrong. He seemed to be asking and answering his
own questions:

—Has she asked about it?

—Nothing makes her happy.

—Not everybody's good at sharing.

—Wait and see?

—Better get back to it.

Before Lily had time to retreat to the opposite end of the
kitchen, the man emerged from the darkness—Oren.

"Oren," she said. "I was just looking for you."

"Were you?" he said, obviously distracted. He took her in
his arms and kissed her forehead. She could smell corn liquor on
his breath. So the jug was out after all. "I was hiding," he said. "I
needed a minute alone. What did you want?"

"More bread," she said. "Was there any in there?"

"No," he said. "The pantry's completely cleaned out."

They stood facing each other, not knowing what to say next.
Ian materialized from the darkness, bearing a loaf of bread.

Oren snatched it from him. "I'd better see what's left of that
ham," he mumbled and made for the dining room.

Ian grinned. Lily could tell by the glassiness of his gaze that
he too had been nipping. A ripple of relief washed over her. She
did not begrudge the twins their moments alone, especially if Ian
needed to complain about Hallie. They had spent so much of
their lives in each other's company—learning how to walk and
talk and work, working side-by-side, lying next to each other in

bed at night—and there were so few moments to be alone these days.

"What's in your pocket?" Lily asked, pointing to the bulge in the front of his good trousers.

Ian produced one of the ornaments from the tree, a wicker basket filled with mistletoe. He held it up over Lily's head and bent down to kiss her. But before his lips met hers, they both heard the squeak of the kitchen door. Lily's father stumbled into the room.

"Daddy!" Lily cried. "You haven't been at the jug, too! I was just scolding Ian here for nipping behind the back of his new wife."

Lily's father grinned sheepishly and scratched behind his ear.

"I was looking for the both of you," he said. "Where the hell is the fiddle music?"

"I guess I kind of forgot," Ian said.

"I'm not talking about them church songs you were playing earlier," her father said. "I'm talking about a reel or two before I fall asleep from politeness."

"I'll go get my rig," Lily said, relieved for the escape. But a thought struck her as she went to fetch her fiddle: what if Ian hadn't been complaining about Hallie? What if it hadn't been Ian speaking at all—what if it had been Oren? You couldn't tell their voices apart unless you were in the same room with them.

But dancing was not to be, not at this party. As soon as some of the menfolk pushed back the furniture in the parlor and began rolling up the rug, Hallie stepped forward to say that, as much as she liked a jig herself, it was getting late. The womenfolk all nodded approvingly and collared their husbands. There were the evening chores in the barn to think about, the morning milking. Coats were fetched, carriages were drawn up. No one could remember a nicer gathering in such a long time. Why didn't they all get together more often? Before Lily quite realized it, the party was over.

Around the new year, Lily received a letter from the Board of Selectmen. Lily's replacement at the library had not worked out as well as anticipated. The Board had, upon further reflection, been hasty in their judgment of Lily's performance—modern times called, no doubt, for a more modern approach to time-keeping. Would Lily possibly consider reapplying for her old position? Lily pretended to deliberate for a couple of weeks and then accepted. She missed her job. There wasn't enough for both Hallie and her to do around the house. Hallie's verbal lists of the chores she needed to perform, the dresses she would sew, the house her husband would build for her when he finally got a moment, were really beginning to wear on her. Why hadn't these endless monologues bothered Lily more when she lunched at Hallie's every day, back before she was married? Lily found the thought of spending an entire day away from her enormously appealing.

Hallie's mother had a stroke that next summer, just after the first mowing. One minute she had been hanging the washing out on the line, the next she had crumpled, with the sheets, into the clover. Hallie's father hadn't found her until he returned from the fields for lunch. Old Doc Perry said there wasn't much he could do. Farming was a hard life and these things happened. Nor was he sure how permanently her right arm and the right side of her face would be paralyzed. Only time would tell that. Hallie's mother would be bedridden, though, until she recovered her strength.

Hallie, an only child, had little choice but to move back in with her parents to care for them.

Before taking leave of The Knoll, she roasted both a ham and a turkey for sandwiches, baked four loaves of bread as well as three pies. She wouldn't have her men wasting away to nothing while she was gone, she said. She was more than happy to prepare dinner for them from her parents' place; she could make pot roast and chicken pie, one-dish meals that could be heated up later. All Ian had to do was stop by on his way home from work. Ian told Hallie she had enough to worry about with her mother. He had survived for twenty years on Oren's cooking, he could certainly make it another couple of weeks.

Lily tried not to feel slighted. None of them had even entertained the notion of her stepping in to do the cooking. Of course she could cook, her mother had taught her all the basics; so what if she didn't *enjoy* cooking, like some women. But she held her tongue—until the morning of Hallie's departure, that is, when Hallie promised to come by The Knoll one morning a week to give the place a *proper* cleaning. Lily burst into tears the moment Ian's car pulled out of the yard. Oren laughed when she admitted why. He gathered her up in his arms and swung her around the front porch. Small price to pay, he told her—having Hallie checking up on them once a week—if it kept her away for a good month. They both laughed then, and did a little jig. Oren suggested they make another pot of coffee. Lily followed him to the kitchen, feeling better. A very small price to pay, indeed.

About an hour later, Ian returned to The Knoll. "So what are we doing today?" he grinned.

"Getting the rest of that porch built for Old Man Morgan," Oren said. "And we had better get a move on. He'll be wondering where we are."

"Like hell," Ian said. "It's a beautiful day outside! We're not spending it with Old Man Morgan breathing his rotten breath down our necks. And Lily isn't going to lock herself away in that dusty old library, either. Today we're going to have some fun, goddamnit."

Lily knew better, of course. She had already had enough trouble with the Board of Selectmen for closing unexpectedly. But there *were* extenuating circumstances: Hallie's mother being so poorly, the family needing to pull together at such times. Everybody would understand—surely. Besides, Ian and Oren were in such a good mood, it had been such a long time since the three of them had had any fun, it was such a beautiful day.

Lily packed a picnic lunch, fixing sandwiches from Hallie's ham. She boiled eggs and made potato salad. She threw a couple of ripe tomatoes into the hamper. She didn't bother with pie. Meanwhile, the twins saddled up the horses. Oren secured the hamper, an old quilt, the triangular chessboard and the two fiddle cases to the backs of their saddles. Ian went to the cellar and triumphantly produced two dusty bottles of claret. They each had another cup of coffee on the porch. Then they set off on a nice long ride.

"Where to?" Ian asked. "Take me someplace I've never been before."

"I know a place," Oren said. "Follow me."

Oren led them across the Peacham Farm Road and up into the woodlot skirting the edge of the Willard farm. Lily relaxed into the ride. By taking the old cowpath that paralleled the road, Oren was avoiding as much contact with town as possible. Lily's mind wandered. The vermilion of sumac, the sulfur of pond water, the tang of horse lather, the bickering of crows, the hiss of pine sap onto the forest floor. Her strongest memories were of summer. She had met the twins in summertime. Childhood, for her, was encapsulated in those three months—watching Buster pitch Oren over the paddock fence, building a treehouse in her parents' orchard, guiding the twins along this very path in the opposite direction, to the swimming hole. Why was it that she hadn't bothered to store memories of childhood winters? She couldn't remember a single birthday or Thanksgiving or Christmas.

She realized where Oren was taking them: the abandoned cemetery. Oren explained the story to Ian as they dismounted and unpacked. This was a sacred Indian site. Cabot Fields used to be located just over the hill. The Abenaki kept burning it down until the townsfolk finally moved it. They could lay their blanket here on the moss, he said, and picnic on the graves of all their ancestors, red or white. He explained about the bells, still jangling in among the markers. He remembered everything. He didn't leave out a single detail—except the fact that he had proposed to Lily here.

They opened a bottle of wine and began a game of triangular chess. They drank and played. Their first game seemed endless; they were all out of practice. When the bottle was empty, they lay on their backs listening for bells. There wasn't a breath of wind. In fact, the woods around them were too quiet, empty of animal sounds. Lily peered between the birches overhead. Thunderclouds had begun to gather in the haze. A moment later, the leaves overhead began to rustle. Then the limbs began to sway. She sat up and held out her palm. She felt a drop of rain, then another. She declared their picnic over. Oren insisted it was pine sap from the hemlocks above, but the horses had begun to stamp and roll their eyes. The distant roll of thunder. They all scrambled to pack. Lily stuffed the remains of their lunch into the hamper, Oren dismantled the chess board, Ian rolled the two fiddle cases in the quilt. They saw the first flashes of lightning once they were mounted. Lily suggested they take the road. They would get home twice as fast that way. Though she dreaded the gossip it might provoke, she didn't want the fiddles to get ruined.

The heavens opened just as they reached the edge of town. Oren, who was on the younger mare, whipped her into a canter. Ian's older mare and Lily's stallion took off after Oren, unprompted. Lily cringed as they stampeded down Main Street. Mercifully, Cabot Fields seemed completely deserted. Its townsfolk had had the good sense to get themselves inside before the storm. The rain lashed at Lily and stung her eyes. Lightning seemed to flash all around. A particularly close crack of thunder frightened her stallion into a full gallop. He overtook Oren's mare and left Ian's in a spray of gravel. It wasn't until the stallion turned into their yard that Lily realized she was laughing. She had been laughing like a lunatic the entire, crazy ride home.

The twins were just as exhilarated when they turned up at the corral a moment later. By then the storm had passed, though they were all soaked to the skin and speckled with mud. Lily began to laugh all over again. The twins joined in, shivering and dripping. They unsaddled the horses and turned them loose. They made their way, chuckling, to the house. Oren built a fire in the parlor and they all stripped down to their underwear, hanging their wet clothes over lampshades and chair-backs, whatever was handy. Ian inspected the fiddles—they were fine—while Lily spread a dry quilt in front of the hearth. Oren uncorked the second bottle of wine and they resumed their picnic pretty much where they had left off, arguing over which chess pieces had been where when the storm interrupted them. It was delicious madness, this roaring fire in the heat of summer with all the windows flung wide open. Dusk fell and Lily lit candles. Moths began clinging to the window screens, dozens of green lunas attracted by the light. They were eerie and beautiful, backdropped by a pink-and orange-tinted sky. They reminded her of something. After another bottle of wine from the cellar, Lily grew sleepy. One moment she was listening to Ian play waltzes and watching the moths, the next she was dreaming.

January. Bitter cold. Waking from a fitful sleep. The white-washed walls of her bedroom flickering an eerie pink, room glowing like the inside of an ear. Danger. Dangerous acrid smell of smoke. Jumping out of bed. Lace curtains pink and fluttering. Making for the window. Flames. Flames trapped like diamonds in the frosty panes. No, real flames. The roof of the horse barn a million sparks, sparks swirling and confusing themselves with the icy stars overhead.

Lily bolted upright, out of her dream. Hallie, wild-haired, dripping in the doorway of the parlor, silhouetted in light. "What is going on here?" Hallie was shouting, hands on hips. Lily blinked. She peered around, trying to make sense enough of her surroundings to give Hallie an answer. It was dark in the parlor now. The fire had burned low, the candles had guttered out. Chess pieces and dirty plates, empty wine glasses and damp clothes fringed the edges of the quilt. Wine, music, song. Too much wine. They had fallen asleep on the blanket. Oren had curled himself around her, Ian had curled himself around Oren. Deep satisfying sleep.

"What are you doing back so soon?" Lily asked. She realized instantly that it was neither the right answer, nor the right question.

Hallie whirled on her heels, spraying droplets of water like sparks. They could hear her stalking down the hallway and slamming the front door.

"Shit," Ian said.

"We were sleeping," Lily said, finally coming up with the right answer. But it was too late. Oren and Ian didn't need an explanation.

Hallie had not seen them galloping through town. She had stopped by the library to get a book to read to her mother. But the library had been locked up tight. The old-timers lingering on the front steps had shaken their heads, saying Lily was at it again. Hallie had gotten worried then—that something had gone wrong up at The Knoll. She had waited for Ian to stop by on his way home from work. He hadn't. She had called on a neighbor to look after her mother. She had come right out, on foot, in the rain.

Lily was having coffee at the kitchen table with the twins while Ian related all of this. He had tried to explain everything to Hallie as soon as he had gotten dressed and driven over. Hallie hadn't wanted any of his excuses; her own two eyes worked perfectly well, she said. She had sent him home, refusing to come back to The Knoll. And she wouldn't be coming back until they had gotten a few things straight between them.

"What does she want?" Oren asked.

"She wants her own house," Ian said.

"We've got work lined up through the fall," Oren said, "paying jobs. We can't just stop all that to build her a house."

"I told her that," Ian said. "Meantime, she wants us to divide this one up. Build a small kitchen for the two of us in our half, bolt up the doors in between."

"Tell her to go to hell," Oren said. "We're not doing that."

Lily felt faint. She stood. She needed air. She stumbled out of the room. Oren called after her. She couldn't speak. She just needed to get out. She stumbled down the drive in the dark. She didn't know where she was going, just away. She crossed the Peacham Farm Road to her parents' place. She thought about waking her mother, asking her for advice. But she couldn't bring herself to hear the answers to her own questions. *What it looks like you're getting up to, that's everyone's business, and you can bet your life the town'll be happy to sit in judgment.* She carried on past the house until she reached the back orchard. As she went, she twisted her ankle. She stopped beneath the crab apple where she and the twins had once built a treehouse. There was very little left of it now: a rotted-out platform, the framing of one wall with a window sill, a tattered rope meant for a swing.

She had always seen herself as wanting the simple things in life. As a little girl, it had been her own bedroom. As an unmarried woman, it had been a job that wasn't cooking and cleaning and sewing all day. But the harder she tried to live a simple life, the more she managed to complicate things—to marry a wanderer, to marry a twin, to marry his twin off to her best friend. And why was she always complicating everything in full view of everyone? Why was she dancing naked around a make-believe fire in the woods, dancing a waltz with both her husband and his brother, sleeping with both her husband and his brother. Didn't she want herself to be happy?

She looked up. The clouds were breaking. She could see stars. She didn't know if she could take the town turning against her again. The cold shoulders, the averted gazes. She had never lived anywhere else. She had practically never *been* anywhere else, except to Boston once to fetch Ian back from the military hospital. She turned to make her way home, resolving to do only those things, from now on, that would make her happy.

Oren was waiting up for her in bed, writing in his book.

"Where have you been?" he asked. "I nearly went out of my mind with worry."

"Thinking," Lily said, beginning to undress. She was tired, very, very tired.

"Me too," he said. "I'm sick and tired of Hallie bossing us around, telling us what to do, getting her way all the time. This is our house, not hers and—"

"But that's what I want, too."

"What?"

"I want us to live like normal people."

"What are you talking about?"

"Divide up the house, at least until you can get around to building them another one. Bolt up all the doors. We'll use the front entrance, they can use the back. They can cook out of the caravan until you put in a kitchen for them."

"I can't just divide up this house. It wasn't built that way."

"Please, Oren," Lily said. "If you love me, if you love me at all, you'll just do it and not argue."

She turned to face him, then, in her simple cotton night dress. She willed herself to look directly into his eyes. She held his gaze until she saw something flicker in his pupils. He stowed his book in the bedside table. He shut off the lamp. She crawled into bed beside him. His back was to her. She held him in the dark. For the first time since she could remember, it was she who was holding him.

The doors were bolted, the back staircase was sealed, the caravan was brought home from town and parked on Hallie's and Ian's side of the house. Oren refused to speak to Lily. Weeks passed in utter silence. Hallie continued to care for her mother at her parents' place. She talked plenty, though, dispelling any doubts about their wild ride through town. According to her, the three of them had been visiting her at her mother's place. Lily had suddenly remembered she had left a pot boiling on the stove. They had torn off to The Knoll in a panic. The kitchen had indeed caught fire but, thank goodness, the rain had kept it from spreading before they had arrived to put it out. Not much damage had been done in the end—you couldn't even see it from the outside—and the twins would have it all repaired by the time she got home.

But Hallie actually had one more demand before she would return to their divided house: that the four of them attend church together on Sunday. She wanted the opportunity to chat to her neighbors about the house Ian would be building for her, building in anticipation of the stork paying them a visit during the coming year.

And so Lily found herself sitting, week after week, in the front-row pew of the First Congregational Church of Cabot Fields. For the entire hour, she felt a pair of giant hands gripping her throat and strangling her. The hands of God, Lily's mother would have claimed, a sure sign that Lily needed to examine her conscience and change her ways. As a child, Lily had often tried to follow her mother's example, bowing her head, squeezing her eyes shut, enumerating her many bad habits: fibbing, bossiness, laziness about her chores—her notions. But her mind would soon wander away from self-improvement to what she might get for her next birthday. As an adult, Lily had stopped trying to please God. She had chosen the more sensible path of avoiding places where she might run into Him.

Now she was trying to please Hallie.

Hallie insisted on sitting at Lily's left—the model sisters-in-law—her arm looped through Ian's, clutching his sleeve. Lily weathered the inevitable waves of nausea by bowing her head and closing her eyes as if in prayer. But she wasn't praying. She was counting. Counting the days backward, wishing they added up to any number of nights of love-making while Ian and Hallie were out at the Opera House. But the counting often brought her back to a mad afternoon, the afternoon of thunderstorm and fire and luna moths. For Lily was fairly certain now: the stork would indeed be paying a visit to The Knoll in the coming year. But it wouldn't be to Hallie's side of the house.

6

※

WORKS HARD FOR A LIVING

[1 9 2 7 - 1 9 2 8]

LILY LAY AWAKE, WAITING FOR FAITH. She had had that dream again—the one about the barn burning—and couldn't seem to drift off. She listened for Faith's footsteps. Her daughter usually padded down the hallway, just after first light, to crawl into bed with her and snuggle. Lily rolled over and sighed. She wished, fleetingly, that Faith was still the baby who slept between her and Oren. But Faith was very much a three-year-old girl now, and had her own bedroom. Oren had carved her a bed in the shape of an elephant as part of their negotiations to get her to move into Ian's old room.

Lily listened to the early-morning sounds of late spring: the warble of robins, the chirp of frogs, the sough of cedar boughs against the window. She watched Oren's shoulders rise and fall. She considered waking him and telling him about the dream. It might help her to dismiss it as indigestion, rather than a sign. She couldn't believe that, at twenty-eight, she was still looking for signs and outcomes in nature. But she didn't reach over. She wanted comfort, and his wakeful silence would not help.

Oren hadn't spoken to her in years—or to Ian, or to Hallie—not since they had divided the house. He rarely spoke at all these days, except to clients or employees. In fact, the only person with whom he conversed regularly was Faith. He made most of his needs clear to Lily through her. Faith would tell her when Oren was out of three-penny nails, when a pair of his work overalls needed mending, when they were invited to her parents' for supper.

Lily had at first pleaded with him to talk. He had merely walked away or turned his back. She tried fighting fire with fire next and, as a result, they had spent much of Lily's pregnancy in complete silence. But then Faith was born, and Oren held his daughter's little hand and whispered into her tiny ear that he loved her more than anything. And Lily had finally understood: it wasn't that Oren wouldn't speak to her; he just couldn't—similar to Ian's shell shock after the war. He couldn't speak because he was terrified, maybe, that he would not be able to stop, that all his pent-up rage would come gushing out, and that he would utter what was on both of their minds: that Lily's giving in to Hallie had ruined their lives. With this understanding came acceptance. Lily allowed Oren his silence. They began to play chess again—ordinary chess. They made love every now and then. He was never abusive to her, never inattentive. The three of them spent a lot of time together, probably more than most families did. He just didn't speak. It was never unpleasant—just very, very quiet. In short, they were not unhappy. But that, she knew, was not the same thing as being happy.

The door creaked open and Faith finally tiptoed in. She was clutching the old tabby Oren had given her as a baby. The cat was a battle-scarred brute about half her size, but he adored her. Faith pitched him up onto the bed. Lily raised the quilt and both little girl and cat crawled under the covers.

"Shh," Faith whispered to the tabby, who was purring crazily. "You'll wake Daddy."

Lily tickled her daughter's belly, causing her to squirm and giggle. Oren silenced them both by rolling over and wrapping his long arms around them. The cat continued to purr beneath the blankets. Lily felt Oren's growing erection on her buttocks. She smiled and closed her eyes. Maybe she would sleep now, if only for an hour . . .

When she woke again, she was alone in bed. She could smell coffee brewing. It must be late. She stretched luxuriously, allowing her toes to explore the cool recesses of the sheets. It had been ages since Oren had fixed his own breakfast—not since Faith was born. A glance at the alarm clock told her she was very late indeed. The old-timers would be lined up and grumbling outside the library if she didn't hurry. These days, she prided herself on her punctuality. She threw off the quilt and hopped out of bed. Instead of feeling panicked, though, she felt exhilarated, as if she had just made love. She should sleep in more often.

"Morning, Sleepyhead," Faith greeted her in the kitchen. "Daddy made me porridge."

"Did you save me any?" Lily asked, kissing her forehead.

"Daddy wanted to eat his with you," Faith said. "I'm going to get dressed all by myself because I'm a big girl now."

"So you are," Lily said. "What will you wear?" She didn't know whether to feel disappointed by missing out on this morning ritual or excited about having breakfast alone with her husband.

"You'll see," Faith said. "I might surprise you." With that she flounced out of the room and clambered up the stairs.

Oren set two bowls of steaming porridge on the table. He poured Lily a cup of coffee and refilled his own. They ate, as usual, in silence, but the quiet was warm and sleepy, not cold and wakeful. Lily sipped her coffee and listened to the noises next door. Normally, she was so busy scrambling eggs and dressing Faith that she didn't hear Ian and Hallie. She often forgot that they too were getting up, eating their breakfast, living their lives on the other side of the wall.

Relations were all but severed with them—especially after Ian had left Pritchard Brothers. He had decided to open a stables instead, if Oren would allow him to buy the horses and barn with his share of the business. Oren had posed no objection and Ian's livelihood had become horses: giving riding lessons, offering stud services, selling tack, caring for the horses of out-of-town neighbors. Hallie planted her own vegetable garden and rosebushes. Lily stocked her own kitchen and hung her own clothes line. Ian now mowed the back lawn and Oren clipped the hedges out front; Ian painted the barn, Oren the house. Over time, the two couples had collectively adopted such a keen sense of avoidance that they rarely ever saw each other, living daily life in syncopated rhythms.

Except for church on Sunday. They were still keeping up appearances.

There was a sudden squeal on the other side of the wall, followed by laughter. Clomping around, like farmhands dancing. Lily raised an eyebrow over her coffee mug. Oren shrugged noncommittally. The moment was interrupted by Faith, entering the kitchen in the first outfit of her career as a big girl: overalls, a pink dress blouse and a crooked red ribbon in her hair. "Well, what do you think?" she asked, placing her hands on her hips the way Lily often did.

"You look beautiful," Lily said. She meant it.

Soon it was time for Oren to leave for work. Lily packed him a lunch and ushered him out the door. He had never been busier, even without Ian. Lily's two younger brothers now worked full-time. The new Pritchard Brothers. They were still running two crews, still prosperous, still not unhappy. Next it was time for her and Faith to wend their way down the drive to the Peacham Farm Road. At the front door, Lily found an unaddressed envelope. Hallie. There must be something wrong with the plumbing or a leak in the roof—a repair that couldn't be handled separately. Reason for all that racket earlier? She tucked the envelope into her coat pocket. Too beautiful a morning to spoil it with one of Hallie's terse notes. The scent of lilacs in the air. They stopped, as they did every morning, to treat Ian's horses to sugar cubes. When they finally reached the mailbox, Lily bent down to give her daughter a hug.

"Tell Granny I'll be a little late today," she said. "I need to pick up a few groceries at the store."

"Be good," Faith said.

"No, you be good," Lily said. She made as if to take the right into town. But she stopped after a couple of paces to watch Faith cross the road and skip up the gravel drive to her mother's kitchen. Just like a normal little girl, Lily thought, spending the day with her grandmother while her mother tended to the town library. Anyone would think she came from a perfectly normal family. And yet. And yet Faith's parents had never spoken one word to each other in her presence. And yet she had only ever seen half the interior of her own house, a place filled with locked doors to mysterious rooms occupied by strangers. And yet she fed her uncle's horses every morning, sat on her aunt's lap at church. Lily dreaded the day Faith would start school. Suddenly she would realize the truth: that very little about her life was normal.

Lily unlocked the library and pulled up the shades. She set her lunch on the table in the back room and filled the kettle for tea. Then she began reshelving the books that had been returned through the door slot after closing. She used to love her job. Now she found a day in the library's cramped maze of bookcases endless. Reshelve books, send overdue notices, help old-timers find yet more titles about Civil War battles, eat a sandwich on the town common, help children with their book reports, write the occasional letter for an illiterate farmer. She hated being away from Faith so many hours. And she worried obsessively about what sort of picture of the world her mother was giving her daughter: what little girls did and did not do. She had asked the Board of Selectmen to begin looking for another librarian shortly after Faith was born. In almost four years there hadn't been a single candidate to interview. The town didn't want to give just anyone that position, she was told whenever she asked. Remember the last time. The town liked things just the way they were.

Half an hour before closing, Lily suddenly remembered Hallie's note. She retrieved the envelope from her pocket and opened it. The loopy script of Hallie's handwriting gave her an instant chill. She read the note quickly, then reread it, letting the words sink in:

> We're moving out. Your brother is selling us a piece of his land across the road. We've bought a nice little house out of the Sears Roebuck catalogue. It should arrive by rail at the end of the month. We intend to keep running the stables, of course. Let us know if this poses a problem.   H.B.P.

Lily tucked the note back into her coat pocket. Air. Would she make it through the final twenty minutes until closing without screaming? Distraction was what she needed. She went to the stacks to find a new book for Oren. Concentrate on that. Oren had become an obsessive reader in his silence, staying up late, devouring book after book by lamplight. He liked just about everything, though he was particularly interested in classical architecture, the Federal style and the craft of building. He had already read all the books Lily's branch owned on the subject. She was waiting on a special order from the library in Montpelier. The minute-hand

crept slowly to twelve. Finally, it was five o'clock. She chose two
biographies, one on Bullfinch, the other on Palladio. She stuffed
them into her bag and announced loudly that the library was closing. She ushered all the old-timers out, turned off the lights,
locked the door and headed for her mother's house.

Usually Faith was playing in her parents' front yard with
Lily's brother's daughter. She had been born perfectly healthy
the year before Faith, in spite of Lily's odd vision of stran-
gulation, and the two of them were now fast friends. Tonight,
though, the yard was empty. The staccato of hammering drew
Lily to the back orchard. She half-expected to find her father
building a new hive. She was not prepared to discover Oren and
Faith up in the old crab apple, tearing up the rotten floorboards
of the abandoned treehouse. Lily's heart leapt into her throat.
There was something about this tree, something from childhood that she couldn't quite remember. Not that that mattered
now. A three-year-old should not, in any case, be climbing rickety
ladders.

Lily set her bags of groceries down next to her father's hives.
She felt confused for a moment—the buzzing of all those insects
inside, swarms of them—but she must tell Faith to be careful. She
cupped her hands to her mouth. Her call was preempted by the
sound of singing. She dropped her hands to listen. Oren's voice,
the first time she had heard it aloud in months. He was teaching
Faith the words to that old nursery rhyme, the one she had first
taught the twins when they were nine, and then retaught them the
afternoon of the snow angels:

> *Wednesday's child is in the know*
> *Thursday's child has far to go*
> *Friday's child is loving and giving*
> *Saturday's child works hard for its living*

Lily drew closer. There, under the tree, was Oren's child-hood tool box, sitting next to his adult one. Faith was wielding a miniature hammer, the one Oren's father had made for him. She was safe. Safe and, no doubt, deliriously happy. She had discovered the treehouse earlier that spring and had asked Oren about it at breakfast. He had explained how they all began building it as children. Faith found it outrageous that they would abandon such a project before it was finished. She had been hounding him to help her repair it ever since. Oren had put her off, promising her someday, someday when he was less busy. Apparently today was someday.

Faith saw Lily and waved.

Lily waved back. "Nearly quitting time, isn't it?" she said. "I don't know about you two but I'm hungry as a bear."

"Me too!" Faith shouted. "I've been working awful hard, haven't I, Daddy?"

Oren looked down at Lily and winked.

"Well then, I wonder what Daddy's going to cook for us," Lily said.

When would she tell Oren about the letter in her pocket? He deserved to know. His brother was moving out. She had no idea whether this would make him happy or sad—or furious. But she would not show him the letter tonight. Oren would cook for them, she knew it. He hadn't cooked in years, not since Hallie moved to The Knoll. He would roast one of his chickens, even though it was warm outside and would be sweltering in the kitchen while they ate it. Maybe Oren would pop the cork on a bottle of wine, something else he hadn't done in ages. The bottle would be covered in cobwebs from the cellar. But wine keeps. It would feel good, like he was coming out of his shell shock. Or if not, it would at least feel like old times. Today was someday. Let the letter wait until tomorrow.

—

Lily didn't show it to him the next day. Or the next. But then Sunday was upon them. They would have to attend church, as usual, with Hallie and Ian. There would surely be a discussion in the car. She approached Oren after breakfast, while he was donning his good clothes. She figured she risked little; a dark cloud had already settled over his good mood.

It was at the limit of what either of them could bear—this weekly hypocrisy of sitting next to Ian and Hallie in a pew at the front. The model family. Hallie's performance was particularly galling. She would adopt an expression of pious serenity as she lured Faith into her lap. She would then hug Faith close as she recited her prayers in a rapturous whisper, stroke the little girl's hair thoughtfully while she pondered the Reverend's sermon, kiss the back of her head when it was time to murmur amen.

"You'd better read this," Lily said, giving Oren the note. He recognized the handwriting and sat on the edge of the bed. A moment later, he handed the note back. He began knotting his tie, though his eyes had filled with tears. "So what do we do?" Lily asked, hoping he would have an answer. Oren shrugged and left the room.

Ian had already pulled his car around to the front when Lily, Oren and Faith stepped out onto the front porch. Hallie opened her door and Faith skipped over to climb into her aunt's lap. Hallie had begun to bribe her with pennies—a penny there, a penny to sit quietly in her lap throughout service, and a penny back. Faith had a growing jar of them in her bedroom. Her plan was to buy a pony of her own one day. Lily and Oren climbed into the back seat. But it wasn't until they were nearly to town that Hallie cleared her throat and said, "You got my note, I'm assuming?"

"We did," Lily said.

"It's time."

"There's no rush," Lily said. She couldn't think of anything else.

"It's time," Hallie repeated. "We'll be holding a house raising. You have to assemble all the pieces—the house comes in pieces. You'll probably want to turn up. For appearance's sake."

"It's a fine little house," Ian broke in. "I'll leave the catalogue on the porch so you can have a look."

A moment of silence.

"So we can count on you at the raising?" Hallie said.

"We'll be there," Lily said.

"Then it's settled," Hallie said.

Lily wasn't sure what had been settled. But any thought of further discussion flew out of her mind as soon as they parked in the church lot and Hallie hoisted herself out of the car. She was wearing a maternity dress.

Lily sat stupefied in the pew. She couldn't look at Hallie for fear of catching her eye. She couldn't look at Oren for fear of what emotion she might discover on his face. Instead, she tried to make sense of this store-bought and expensive dress. So Hallie was not, contrary to common belief, getting fat from a life of indolence. She was a good four or five months along. That she had never gotten pregnant by her first husband was understandable. But several years of marriage to Ian without children had lulled Lily—like everyone else—into assuming that Hallie was barren.

At the end of service, when it was time to greet friends and neighbors with the customary handshake, Hallie turned to Lily, as usual, to kiss her cheek. Lily had to admit she looked radiant. She took Hallie's hand into her own and murmured congratulations. She hadn't planned on doing this; the gesture was spontaneous. Hallie leaned forward and brushed her lips against Lily's ear. "Go to hell," she whispered. Then she turned to the neighbors in the pew behind.

After that, Lily was firm. She made Faith sit in the back of the car with her and Oren, in spite of her whining and begging. Lily might be forced to watch Hallie's belly grow rounder and her breasts more ample with each passing Sunday. She might have to endure Hallie's smugness and suffer all her false kisses. But now she drew the line where it concerned her daughter. There would be no more pennies.

A few weeks later, another note on the porch. Hallie's and Ian's new house had arrived at the train station. A raising was scheduled for the following Saturday. With the note was a Sears, Roebuck catalogue of *Honor-Bilt Modern Homes*. Lily thumbed through it as she made breakfast for Oren and Faith. It boasted more than one hundred ready-to-assemble houses, cottages and garages in the "bungalow style." The names of the kit houses all sounded familiar: Sumner, Savoy and Belmont; Hampton, Somerset and Wellington—names right out of Mr. Pritchard's worn copy of *Payne's Encyclopedia of Rural Residences*. Yet these so-called bungalows bore no resemblance whatsoever to Payne's elegant classical designs and symmetrical layouts.

Page 37 had been dog-eared and given a big red star: The Sheridan, Model No. 3334. A squat two-story cabin with oversize eaves, tiny windows, a wide front porch and virtually no other ornamentation. Of course Ian had chosen The Sheridan over all the others, in spite of its boxy little rooms and awkward floor plan. Lily wondered if Ian had shared the real reason with Hallie. She smiled grimly. Another secret binding the three of them together. She set the catalogue next to Oren's glass of orange juice. Then she sat in his chair and stared at it, so overwhelmed was she by missing Ian, missing the three of them, missing home.

—

Lily, Oren and Faith were among the first to arrive at the building site on Saturday morning. It was their duty. And as Lily expected, the townsfolk began turning up shortly afterward. There hadn't been a house raising all year. And no one in Cabot Fields had ever heard of a house being delivered in pieces on a wagon. The men brought their hammers and saws (they each knew what their finest tool was, intending to show it off as well as use it); the women brought their best potato salad or casserole or pie for the picnic lunch. There wasn't much to see or do, at first. Everyone was milling around the concrete foundtion Ian had poured according to the first instruction manual Sears, Roebuck had sent. To pass the time, they all complimented the land Lily's brother had sold Ian. It was a fine place to build a house—near the road, near the river, facing east. There was no truth in this. Hallie and Ian would be covered in dust in the summer, besieged by mosquitoes in the spring and chilled to the bone in the winter. The compliments were for Hallie's benefit as she waddled among them in another store-bought maternity dress, pouring strong black coffee and passing fresh-baked muffins. Where was Ian? Fetching the house at the railroad station. It had arrived in two boxcars—some thirty thousand pieces in all.

Finally the first wagon arrived. It was piled high with rafters, joists and studs. The men unloaded these, as well as crates containing nails and screws, paint and varnish, knobs and hinges. There still wasn't much to do except admire the cleverness of the precut and numbered lumber (considerable) and the craftsmanship of the carved mantel and banister (shoddy). But then Ian arrived in the second wagon of fireplace bricks, roofing shingles, and plumbing. He handed out assembly manuals and blueprints and the men set to work. It was slow going, not due to lack of skill—these men had been raising barns and putting additions on houses all their lives—but because every butt end of lumber needed to be checked for a number and matched up to where it appeared on the blueprint. Luckily, more pieces of the house kept arriving throughout the morning to keep the crowd entertained: floorboards and wainscoting, kitchen cabinets and built-in bookcases. The site began to look like a giant jigsaw puzzle.

Lily found herself watching Ian as she drifted among the menfolk pouring them glasses of lemonade or beer. He was carefully avoiding Oren. Whenever Oren moved to the front, Ian made his way to the back; if Oren was framing a wall, Ian dove under the floorboards to examine the piping. She remembered when the two of them were building The Knoll—how each had anticipated the movements of the other. Their natural rhythm had reminded her of a dance. Now they didn't speak. How could they stand it? She watched Hallie sidle up to Ian. Ian set his hammer down and took Hallie into his arms. He held her close, he kissed her forehead, he rubbed her belly. Lily flushed with rage. How could Ian bear to touch her—after all Hallie had done! Hallie had gotten everything she had ever wanted, at everyone else's expense: a husband who bent to her every whim, a little house of her own, a baby on the way.

It got worse. At lunch, Lily was stationed at the buffet table with Hallie and the other farm wives. Women were always relegated to serving lemonade, minding the children, dishing out food. She couldn't think of anything more excruciating than standing around listening to their insults masked as compliments. *That's such a pretty dress! Of course, I could never wear that color myself . . . Wasn't the Grange dance wonderful? Oh but you left early, didn't you, with your husband's cousin? I hope you weren't ill . . .* She spooned out potato salad and watched the men eat their lunch. Men spoke a frank language with their bodies that she admired. She assumed this was because their focus was outside of themselves, on joining up the various elements of the house, on fitting the pieces of a puzzle together—on play. Whereas a woman's focus was always a reflection of herself: how her beauty had won over the most handsome bachelor in town, how her cleverness with figures had saved the farm during a crop failure, how her long suffering would one day be rewarded in heaven. It was the difference, Lily supposed, between having your sex outside or in.

"I don't know how my husband finds the time," Hallie was commenting to Lily's sister-in-law. "He's got more horses stabled in that barn than he can possibly take care of. And yet he takes all this on."

"There's a family to think about now," her sister-in-law replied.

Hallie smiled and smoothed the front of her dress to accentuate her swelling stomach. "She's going to be her father's pride and joy."

"You think it'll be a girl, then, Hallie?"

"I do."

"What's this I hear about Ian becoming a deacon at the church?"

"Now, Reverend Higgins only asked Ian if he would *consider* it."

"That's not what I hear. Anyway, what with the stables and the church and all your committees and charity work, Hallie, it sounds like the both of you will have your hands full. You thinking about getting some help in?"

"Oh no," Hallie said. "I'll stop with all I'm doing for the church. My place will be at home with my daughter. I can't have her running around and growing up half wild—"

Lily slammed her serving spoon down on the table and strode away. She found Oren, pulled him aside and told him she wasn't feeling well; she needed to go home. He furrowed his brow, put the back of his hand to her forehead to feel for fever. It's not that, she said. She started to cry. She turned away and began walking. Oren followed her. Don't, she said, it'll draw attention. I'll be fine. He insisted on walking her home.

It all came pouring out. She told him she was sorry, sorry that she had made such a disappointing wife, that she was a terrible mother, that their daughter ran wild. She was sorry about ruining their happiness by orchestrating Ian's marriage to Hallie. And she was truly sorry that she would no longer be able to keep her end of the bargain. But she could not possibly bring herself to set foot inside that church another Sunday. Oren would have to take Faith to service on his own. And the town would just have to think what it would think.

Oren sat them both down on the front porch swing. He placed her head in his lap and stroked her hair while she cried herself out. They rocked together in silence for a good long while, rocking, rocking and staring at Ian's Sears, Roebuck house. Eventually Oren stood. But instead of heading back to the raising, he went inside. She heard his boots clomping up the stairs. She closed her eyes. She was so weary. When he returned to the porch, he was carrying his small, leather-bound book. He leafed through its pages, found what he was looking for, and held it out to her, open. Childish, block print. He had never learned to write in cursive. She knew the book, of course. Often he wrote in it before bed. He kept it in the drawer of the bedside table. She had never peeked inside. She understood the need for privacy.

"You want me to read this?" she asked.

He nodded.

"But just this bit here, not the whole book."

He nodded again, then shrugged. He bounded down the porch steps.

"I'll put it back when I'm done," she called after him.

He smiled and waved. She watched him return to Ian's

house raising. He was a good man. He would help with the raising though he and his brother weren't speaking. He would dance at the party afterward to keep up appearances. He would collect Faith from the women minding the children so that she wouldn't have to face Hallie again. Lily vowed to bake him something special and leave it on the kitchen counter for when he got home. She felt the weight of the open book in her lap.

> They say Charles Bullfinch spread the Federal style of architecture throughout New England. That's not true. It was the ordinary housewright. There wouldn't be a Salem, Massachusetts without Samuel McIntyre. Most of Bennington, Vermont owes a debt to Lavius Fillmore. Orford, New Hampshire was built by my grandfather. They passed what they knew, along with their pattern books, down to their sons. I have no sons. Now my brother has left me. I am the very last housewright. When I'm gone, people will just start buying their houses out of the Sears Roebuck catalogue. What will New England look like then?

Just when you thought you knew someone. Lily felt a confusion of emotions: surprise at the intellectual nature of Oren's prose (she was expecting a log of accounts); pride in his native intelligence (though his handwriting was atrocious); sadness about the pain his break with Ian was obviously causing him. What could be more insulting for a housewright, after all, than to have his own brother buy a home out of catalogue? She closed the book. She didn't think she could bear any more at the moment. She would return it to the drawer.

She slept badly that night. And she woke with a feeling of dread in the pit of her stomach. How would she explain to Faith that they would no longer be attending church with Uncle Ian and Aunt Hallie? Or would Oren still take her—to keep up appearances? By breakfast, it was clear he had no intention of doing this. He turned up at the table in his overalls, smiling and holding out his cup for coffee. It dawned on Lily then that keeping up appearances had been her idea all along. It was she who had wanted to live a "normal" life; not he. Faith also came to breakfast in her overalls. Oren had obviously explained everything to her, perhaps over brownies and milk the night before. For she did not once mention changing into her good clothes or riding into town in the car. Her chatter careened from the house-raising to the games she had played with her cousins, to how she would grow up to be a carpenter one day, to the afternoon ahead of building her new treehouse. Her interest in church had clearly been about the pennies.

Later, when Lily was hanging the sheets out on the line to dry, she heard Ian's car pull around to the front. Three impatient blasts of the horn. A minute or two of silence. Three more blasts. More silence. More silence. She smiled. She pegged another pillowcase to the line.

They didn't know what to do with the empty half of The Knoll. By now they had grown used to living in their own side. They decided to keep the doors bolted, just as before, until they figured it out. And so it sat empty for most of the summer. Oren eventually moved some of his tools into Hallie's and Ian's back parlor and set up a woodworking shop. Lily avoided going over there unless it was absolutely necessary. She would rap her shoe against the wall when it was time for Oren to come to supper.

One night in Indian Summer, just before bed, Lily was getting a glass of water in the kitchen and heard scuffling next door. A family of raccoons had been tearing up the last of her kitchen garden. She worried that they had decided to take up residence in the empty part of the house. She debated whether she should call Oren down from the bedroom to have a look. She scolded herself for being such a coward—she had lived on a farm all her life and, besides, it was probably a loose shutter—but she took a broom with her, just in case.

Once she was next door, however, she realized she should also have brought a lantern. She couldn't remember where any of the gas lamps were. She stood in the middle of Hallie's kitchen and listened, waiting for her eyes to adjust to the gloom. Nothing. She felt her way down the corridor into the front parlor. Nothing. She was just about to turn back when she heard rustling in Ian's and Hallie's old bedroom. She groped her way over to the door and swung it slowly open as she raised her broom. She started. Something larger than a raccoon was huddled in the bay window where the bed should have been. Ian.

Lily lowered her broom. Everyone knew you shouldn't wake sleepwalkers. But Lily realized now that she didn't know *why*. What was worse: waking him, or letting him catch pneumonia on those filthy hardwood floors? She tiptoed over and crouched beside him. She lay a hand on his shoulder. She shook him gently. "Ian," she whispered, "wake up."

She saw his eyes open. They glinted in the moonlight. He stared at her, unseeing. "Where the hell am I?" he whispered.

"It's Lily."

"What are you doing here?" Ian said.

Lily giggled. "You were sleepwalking. You're at The Knoll."

Ian sat up. He rubbed his eyes. He looked around. "I'd better be getting back," he said. "Hallie will be worried."

"No wait," Lily said, sitting next to him. "Stay just a minute and talk."

"About what?"

"Oren misses you. Talk to him. I'm sure the two of you can work something out."

"We have talked. We worked it all out. We decided it's best this way."

Lily was stunned into silence. When had they talked? When had they seen each other? Why hadn't Oren told her? Why wouldn't he talk to her? Ian stood. He dusted off his pajamas. He held his hand out to help her to her feet. She took it. They stood in the darkness, holding hands. She didn't want him to go.

"But why should Hallie always get to have her way?" she sobbed.

Ian dropped her hand. He stared at her intently, his eyes glittering. He turned to leave the room. Lily watched him go, sobbing silently. "What's Hallie got to do with it?" Ian whispered over his shoulder.

Lily wiped her eyes with her fists. She followed him out. She decided to tell Oren it was raccoons and that he should lay out poisoned corn in the morning.

November of 1927 was the rainiest anyone in Cabot Fields could remember. Not a single day of sun the entire month. A steady downpour that raised every river in Central Vermont to overflowing. It would later become known as The Great Flood, and the old-timers would regale anyone who would listen about how the citizens of Barre canoed around their streets as though they were the canals of Venice, how barns floated down the Winooski River with pigs and chickens still in them, how families moved up to their attics and lived there on dried corn and field mice until the waters finally fell. People's whole lives were swept away overnight, the old-timers would say. But people always came back, always rebuilt.

The last Saturday of November barely dawned, and the rain continued to slash against the window panes of The Knoll. Lily peered out the parlor bay at the expanse of water separating her from her parents' house. The creek at the bottom of her property was creeping up to the Peacham Farm Road. Oren and Faith had left for town right after breakfast to get milk and flour before the way became impassable. It made Lily nervous that Oren was driving in such terrible weather. She herself was meant to be at her mother's house helping out with the annual Christmas cooking. There were gift fruitcakes to cure in brandy, meat pies to make and freeze for Christmas Eve, sugar cookies to bake and have on hand for any friends or relatives who stopped by. As usual, Christmas would not be celebrated at The Knoll. Lily's parents' party would be more than enough merry-making for them.

Lily put on her galoshes, marveling at how much easier the newfangled "zippers" were than buttons. She retrieved her coat from the closet and tied a scarf over her hair. She left the house reluctantly and began crab-walking her way down her rutted and runneled drive. She was just passing Hallie's and Ian's house when she heard what sounded like the howl of a wolf. She was so startled, she slipped in the mud and landed heavily on her hip. She lay there for a moment, wondering if she had hurt anything. Before she could check, she heard another cry. A human scream, Hallie's scream, coming from inside the house. She stood and limped over to the porch. She hadn't broken anything, though she would probably be bruised the following day. She tried the door. It wasn't locked. She let herself in.

"Hallie?" she called from the front hall. Silence. All she could hear was the drum of rain on the roof. "Hallie, it's Lily. Are you all right?" She waited, wondering if the noise had been a wolf or coyote after all. Suddenly a low keening moan echoed down the staircase. "Hallie are you up there?" She didn't know her way around this house. She had never been invited in.

"Go away," Hallie moaned. Another scream.

Lily bounded up the stairs, forgetting for the moment about her fall. She found Hallie in her nightgown, lying on a blood-soaked bed. She was drenched with sweat and as white as the pillow-cases propping up her matted head. "I said go away," Hallie panted when she saw Lily. "It's too early. I'm not supposed to be having her for another month yet."

"For Pete's sake, Hallie, you look like you're bleeding to death."

"Go away. It's not time yet." She was delirious.

Lily dropped her coat on the floor and went to check Hallie's forehead. She was burning up. "Lift up your legs, Hallie," Lily said. "I need to see how far along you are." Surprisingly, Hallie did as she was told. Lily mopped at the blood with the edge of the top sheet. She could plainly see the baby's head. There was not really enough time to get a doctor. Why on earth were Hallie's legs down? "You've got to keep these propped up and sepa-rated," Lily told her. "Like this. Now I'll be right back. I'm just going to get a basin of water."

There wasn't time to boil the water. Hallie's screams were getting more and more frequent. She grabbed some fresh towels out of the laundry basket in the kitchen, hoping they weren't Hallie's good ones. She bounded up the stairs two at a time.

The next half hour had the quality of a dream. Lily felt as though she had detached herself from her own body and was hov-ering above it, watching it as it worked feverishly to bring Hallie's baby into the world. She could see herself crouching between Hallie's splayed legs with her sleeves rolled up, trying to get a pur-chase on the baby's head. Keep those legs up, she kept having to remind Hallie. And push, goddamnit; you're not pushing hard enough! Hallie screaming and groaning, grunting, grunting.

Telling Lily to go away in one breath, begging her for help in the next. It all felt so familiar, this scene, as if she had already lived it. And the worst of it was, she already knew how it would end. The baby would finally plop out of Hallie's womb in a gush of blood. It would lie still on the sheets—strangled by its own umbilical chord, lifeless. No, please no, Lily kept chanting to herself, over and over again. Please no.

But all too soon possibility became the present. It sputtered briefly in Hallie's stifling bedroom—hope—before becoming the past. Hallie's plight was over. Hallie's misfortune. Lily cut the blue lifeless body out of its noose with a pair of Hallie's sewing scissors and wrapped it in a towel. Exhausted, Hallie panted, "Girl or boy? Let me see it, Lily. I need to know if it's a little girl or a little boy." Lily didn't. She told Hallie to sit tight; she was just going to put the kettle on. She took the bundle out of the room with her. She set it on the kitchen table. She went to find Ian in the horse barn.

The next day, Oren began working on a coffin in his workshop. Lily left him alone, though his wood plane seemed to cut into her with every scrape. She packed Faith off to her mother's for the day. It didn't seem like the proper thing for a little girl to be around. Feeling useless, Lily tried to get ahead of the housework. But in spite of her dusting and bed-stripping and sheet-washing, she was keenly aware of Oren's intervals of measuring and sawing, cutting all the boards he needed to the right size. Sound carries through wood.

Just before lunch, she heard the syncopation of two saws. Curiosity got the better of her. She made a fresh pot of coffee. She brought it and two cups over to Oren's workshop on the other side. Of course it was Ian. He had brought his own tool box. They were working in complete silence, side by side. Lily left the pot of coffee outside the door. She tapped on the window pane and then beat a hasty retreat to her kitchen.

She brought them a late lunch. Sandwiches and hardboiled eggs, large wedges of chocolate cake, more hot coffee. This time she brought the tray inside and set it down among the pine shavings on the workbench. They were now dressing all the boards they had cut. Neither of them looked up, so intent were they on their work. Lily wanted to rush over, place an arm around both of their waists and hug them to her. Instead, she turned to go. "You don't have to leave, Lily," Ian said. She turned back. She looked around for a chair. She perched on the edge of the workbench. Oren kept planing; he was taking comfort in the work. But Ian wandered over. He wanted to talk. "Look at all the planes our father had," he said, fanning his hand over the tools on the bench. "A jack plane for rough work, short and long jointers for dressing, half a dozen smoothing planes. Some of these blade frogs are so fine you can see light through the shavings they make."

Lily didn't know what to say. She handed Ian a sandwich. Ian bit into it right away. But he continued talking as soon as he had swallowed. "Our father's fingertips were so sensitive that he could tell when a wainscoting plank was badly ripped, just by running his thumb along the edge," he said. "He'd tell the sawyer it was a quarter-inch too thick three-quarters of the way down. The sawyer would tell him he was crazy—until he got the yardstick out."

Lily poured him a cup of coffee. She raised the pot at Oren, questioningly. Oren shook his head no. She set it down on the workbench.

"He started us out on coffins when we were four," Ian continued, inspecting one of the planks he had finished. "Perfect practice, now that I think of it. Coffins require all the skills of woodworking. There's always plenty of them to make. And no one ever complains when the corners aren't true or the carving's bad." He turned to Oren. "Eat something. There's hours of work ahead. I need this to be one of our finest."

Oren stopped what he was doing. His eyes welled. He nodded and came to the bench for a sandwich. Ian took a sip of coffee. He set his cup aside and took up two boards, forming a corner edge with them. "The best-made coffins are the plainest," he said. "When you see cherubs dancing around the edges, you know the carpentry is shoddy. A bit of scrollwork does wonders for covering up poorly sawn planks or badly joined edges. We've always tried to do our finest work for children."

"Cake?" Lily asked. Ian nodded. She handed him a plate and a fork. Ian took the slice of cake in his hands. "We don't have anything to line the coffin with," he said between bites.

"I'll find something," Lily said. "What size?"

Oren wrote the dimensions out on a scrap of wood.

"Bring it here," Ian said. "You can work on it here, with us."

"Need anything from the house?" she asked, her voice husky. They shook their heads. "I'll just go and get my sewing kit," she said, gathering up the tray.

The only satin she had in the house was her bridesmaid dress from Hallie's wedding. She would gladly have used her own wedding gown—at least the fabric would be white and not robin's-egg blue—but she had never moved that trunk from her mother's attic. She doubted Ian would recognize the color, but she ripped the seams in her bedroom, just in case. Then she rejoined the twins in the workshop. Oren was assembling the box while Ian carved an elegant beveled cross into the lid. Lily shivered. There was something grotesque about the coffin's miniature size—something inappropriate—as though death were an activity reserved only for grown-ups. Ian stopped to inspect his handiwork. He traced the cross with his fingertips. But he wasn't finished. He flipped the lid over and took up his chisel and mallet again. She watched as he began to carve a small figurine at eye level—a tiny angel. Suddenly Lily was sitting in the treehouse with Oren, their feet dangling over the edge, while Ian carved the very same angel into the tree bark. The place's secret name.

They passed the afternoon like this, in silence, lost in their own thoughts. By nightfall, the coffin was nearly assembled; Lily had had enough material left over to make a little satin pillow.

They all jumped when the door knob rattled. Hallie burst into the room. She was wrapped in a bed quilt instead of a coat, and she looked terrible: her eyes red-rimmed and wild, her face drawn and pale, her hair hanging in loose, oily clumps.

"What are you doing here?" she shouted at Ian.

"You shouldn't be out of bed," Ian said. "I thought your mother was looking after you."

"I can't turn my back one minute without you sneaking off," she said. "Just what in hell do you think you're up to, anyway?"

"What does it look like I'm up to?"

Lily stood. "Come on into the house, Hallie. I'll make you a cup of tea."

"Stay away from me!" Hallie screamed. "Murderer!"

"Shh, now," Lily said, taking a step forward, "don't be saying hurtful things. Just come into the house."

"Get away from me! You killed my baby, you jealous bitch. You ought to be hanged for it."

Lily stopped, stunned. "You know that's not true, Hallie. She was stillborn, strangled on her own cord."

"I saw her! I saw her on the table. There wasn't any cord around her neck. I said as much to Old Doc Perry, too. He knows the truth."

"Stop now," Lily said. "I cut it away before he got there."

"Liar!" Hallie screamed. Her legs buckled then, and she crumpled to the floor.

—

It was bitter cold the day of the funeral. The church ceremony had to be put off a week, until Hallie was strong enough to attend. Not that it mattered, really—the ground was too saturated with flood water for a proper burial. And by the time the rivers had subsided, the ground would be frozen solid. The coffin would have to be stored in the cemetery's mausoleum now until the first thaw. They would all have to go through this again, graveside, at an interment ceremony. Hallie had sent word by her mother that she didn't want Lily or Oren at the funeral. They went anyway, to pay their respects. They just made sure to sit in the back. Hallie didn't even notice them. She wasn't in her right mind.

Weddings and funerals. Lily knew about the gossip, of course. Hallie's mother had been spreading her daughter's mad rantings all over town. She didn't believe Hallie's accusations any more than the rest, not really. Doc Perry had confirmed how it was. He didn't need to see the umbilical cord to know the baby had died in Hallie's body. But it was the middle of winter, and everyone was tired of being cooped up inside. And the story was too delicious not to repeat and repeat and repeat. Besides, everyone had begun to suspect things weren't quite right, up there on the hill. They had all stopped going to church together.

The rustle and whisper of black crepe. The drone of the Reverend's voice. Lily stared at the tiny coffin through the dark forest of familiar heads and shoulders. It gleamed on a small rolling table at the altar, nested in wreaths of tea roses and hothouse lilies. No bigger than a steamer trunk, really. There were four pallbearers, but any reasonable-sized farmer could have lifted it himself. Thank goodness the Burkes were Congregationalists and didn't believe in open caskets.

Lily couldn't blame the town for their talk. She couldn't stop herself from picking over the facts. Why had she cut the umbilical cord away? Why hadn't she waited for Old Doc Perry to get there? Was she absolutely sure the baby was dead when it came out? Why hadn't she tried to blow air into its lungs? That's what all the old wives' tales said to do, everyone knew that.

Hush now. That baby was dead.

Winter dragged on, and Lily dragged herself from one twilight to the next. It was hard on her, knowing that Hallie and her mother were still bad-mouthing her at the post office and general store, telling anyone who would listen that God would be Lily's judge if the law couldn't see fit to investigate the matter further. It wasn't like the waltz at the Grange, though, when she was clearly in the wrong. Oren still had more work than he could handle, even in the dead of winter. People still came by the library to check books out or look up bronchitis remedies. They were always polite, pretending like nothing unusual had happened. But it was exactly that, that no one ever asked Lily for her side of the story, that wore her down. Just when she thought she would go mad from it all—the grayness, the lack of snow, her neighbors' insistence on chatting about the weather—her parents invited her over for supper. No reason, her mother said, we just haven't had a meal together in a while. Faith can help me with the cooking. Bring your fiddle.

Lily didn't feel much like going. She worried it was one of her mother's traps to admonish her during dishwashing about her daughter's behavior. But Faith was excited about making pies with Granny, and Oren had polished up the pieces of his best chess set with linseed oil. So Lily fixed the hem on her old church dress, dusted off her fiddle and across the road they went.

Her father greeted them at the door with kisses and claps on the back. He poured them all a glass of dandelion wine to get things rolling, he regaled them at the supper table with stories

about how naughty he had been as a little boy. His mood was so
contagious that Lily realized, asking for seconds of her mother's
pot roast, she was having a wonderful time. Clearly, this little supper party hadn't been her mother's idea at all. So when her father
asked her, over coffee, to play something nice on her fiddle, she
tried her best. It had been a very long time—a lifetime ago, it
seemed—since she had held the instrument in the crook of her
arm. Faith was utterly enchanted. Somehow, it had never occurred to Lily to tell Faith that she knew how to play. Faith
crowed with delight as Lily tuned the strings and ran through a
few scales to limber up her fingers. Good thing her daughter's ex-
pectations were so low; Lily only knew the melody to a few pieces.
She had always played second fiddle to Ian. But a half-glass of
Canadian Club jogged her courage. And a few of the livelier jigs
came back. Soon her father was on his feet, asking Faith to dance.
By then he had indulged in a snort or two himself. Oren got up
and bowed to Lily's mother. She refused at first, but he would not
take no for an answer. She surprised them all by standing, hiking
up her skirts, and doing a little clog. She stopped just as suddenly,
though, and announced that she needed to see to the supper
dishes. When Lily went to the kitchen to help, she found her
mother crying at the sink. "What's wrong?" Lily asked, alarmed.
They had been having such a nice time.

Lily's mother wiped her eyes with the corner of her apron. "I
miss my boy," she said. "He should be here." Lily gathered her
mother into her arms—for the first time, maybe, in her life. Because she understood.

Only after Lily's father had beaten Oren at a game of chess
would he consent to walk them to the door. By then, Faith had
fallen asleep in Oren's arms. Lily threw her own arms around her
father and hugged him tight. "Thank you, Daddy," she whispered
into his ear. "Just what the doctor ordered."

"Doctor and everybody else knows you were only trying to

help," he whispered back. "Fact is, most of us are damn sick of hearing about it. Hallie's only harming herself now."

Lily nodded. Spring was a few months off yet. But it would come, it would come.

Lily closed the library early the day of the interment. The ground had finally thawed; Hallie's baby could now be buried. Closing the library was the proper thing to do. Lily was family. Neither she nor Oren would be attending the service. For appearance's sake, Oren had also agreed, begrudgingly, to take the afternoon off from work, though he seemed to grow less and less interested in appearances as time wore on. He would spend it with his daughter at the treehouse.

Lily decided to check on them during her walk home. She would ask them what they wanted for supper. Walking felt good. The forsythia had finally cascaded into bloom along the Peacham Farm Road, purple crocuses were peeking up among the rotted maple leaves. Off on the horizon, Mount Mansfield was still gray, but cloaked now in a sheer green veil. Lily found herself breathing deeply—not from exertion, not to fill the emptiness in her heart—more like the expulsion of winter. Air heavily scented with dogwood blossoms and rich black mud, melting brook ice and stone fences warming in the sun.

They were near the trunk of the crab-apple tree when Lily came upon them. Oren was trying to teach Faith how to use his two-man saw. They were so intent on their task that they didn't see her. She suppressed a laugh, watching them. Faith was hanging on to her handle with dogged determination while Oren dragged her back and forth, playing her like a hooked trout at the end of a fly-fishing line. Eventually the difference between their sizes and strengths grew too great and Faith tumbled to the ground. Faith laughed uproariously, Oren chuckled in his usual quiet manner. Faith stood and slapped the sawdust off her overalls while Oren realigned the saw on the plank. They began again. The flutter of apple blossoms all around.

Lily never knew whether she was invited into moments like these, or whether she was meant to watch them from a respectful distance. Either way, her very presence altered them, she knew, transformed them into something different—the next moment— which somehow relegated what she was watching, the passing of her daughter's childhood without her, to the past. Yet Lily stepped forward, she couldn't help herself. The loneliness of watching was too hard. She had been surrounded by people since the day she was born, but had never had a sister. And though she had insisted on having her own room as a little girl, the thing she truly feared the most was finding herself alone.

Faith insisted on showing Lily all the progress they had made that afternoon. Lily followed her up the ladder and inspected the newly refurbished platform as well as the framing of all four walls. Progress indeed, Lily said. As children, they had not gotten much farther than the platform and swing. Oren climbed up to nail a bracing beam into place. The wall wobbled precariously. Lily reminded Faith not to lean on anything until her father told her it was safe. Feeling slightly dizzy, she went to stand closer to the trunk. A thought occurred to her: Ian's angel was carved into the bark somewhere. She looked for it, but couldn't find it. Too much time had passed. She was just about to ask Faith if she had seen it when she heard the whinny of a horse.

Ian was galloping across her parents' back pasture on the stallion. He was wearing his best suit, though the tie had been loosened and his white shirt was now untucked. He didn't seem to notice them as he careened past. Lily could see his face was wet with tears. He didn't slow for the stone wall directly in his path.

He dug his heels into the stallion's flanks to urge him forward. They sailed over the fence—it was a lovely thing to watch—and galloped, horse and man, off in the direction of the woodlot.

Lily's heart went out to him. She knew what it was like to run away from grief. You ran and you ran but, try as you might, it somehow clung to you. She remembered his touch once, in a hayfield of the past. Sadness and frustration, suffocation and anger, acceptance. She wondered how it must feel, to have all this grief, more than any one person should ever have to bear, and not be able to turn to his twin brother, the person with whom he had always shared such things—everything—and not have him there. Watching Ian, she realized how much she loved him. He had always lightened Oren's seriousness with music, diluted his sadness with a joke. Lily turned to Oren now, to gauge his reaction. Oren was following Ian's progress across the pasture with his eyes, oblivious to all else. And even in this terrible moment, he seemed lighter, freer, more himself. But as soon as Ian disappeared into the woods, his features eased back into the dull lines Lily had grown used to reading these past three years. Loneliness. Oren leaned forward and whispered into his daughter's ear. Faith turned to Lily and said, "Daddy wants to know what you think he should do."

Lily was suddenly overwhelmed with rage. Some secret door in her heart opened and it all came pouring out, all the years she had been putting up with—with *this*. "It's not all my fault, you know," she yelled at him. "It's your fault, too. And his. And Hallie's. How the hell should I know what to do next? I never bargained for any of this. I thought I was marrying you, goddamnit. Just you. He's your brother. Why don't you tell *me*. In fact, that's an excellent idea. You tell me, to my face, Oren Pritchard, how you would like me to get us out of this mess. Because I'm, frankly, all out of ideas."

Oren jerked up from where he had been crouching to nail the brace—to get away from her, Lily assumed, which was his tactic whenever she tried to confront him. Walk away, then. And this time keep walking. But one of his legs buckled beneath him and he lost his balance. He clutched at the new wall to right himself. The framing groaned under his weight—it wasn't secure—and something snapped. He was falling.

Lily grabbed Faith's arm and pulled her to the safety of a limb. Time seemed to stop. She watched it all fall away from her: the unfinished walls collapsing and cascading like kindling to the ground, her husband somersaulting backward. Everything falling at once, following her husband. A little girl—not Faith—falling off the hub of a wheel, trying to peer into a tiny house on a wagon. A freckled boy somersaulting naked off a rope, shattering the still surface of a pond. A young woman losing her grip on library shelves and tumbling to the floor in a shower of dusty books. A young woman falling back onto a bed of maple leaves in an abandoned cemetery with maples leaves drifting down all around her. A young woman sinking into a large lap with another set of hands poised over her own to guide them through a waltz. A young woman sinking back into the rumpled sheets of an already occupied bed. Shiny maple chess pieces toppling—rooks and knights— on a hell-bent quest for a queen. A tall and handsome man walking away, running away, galloping away, the very act of walking away to keep from falling . . .

Another snap, the snap of a neck. The slow drift of apple blossoms onto Oren's crumpled, motionless body. Her daughter's high-pitched screams piercing the slow tumbling out of horror. Screams falling to the ground and shattering.

7

✤

FAIR AND WISE AND GOOD

[1 9 2 8]

LILY'S YOUNGEST BROTHER FINALLY CAME OUT to The Knoll to teach her how to drive. It was a Saturday afternoon in late May, and as soon as she saw his old Ford, she sent Faith off to her mother's. Getting her brother to agree to the lessons had taken several weeks of persuading. The women of Cabot Fields didn't drive. They could walk wherever they needed to go. And any-where they *wanted* to go—to the new cinema in Montpelier, to the Tunbridge Fair, or to relatives on the Derby Line—they should be escorted by their men. Lily driving herself around would only cause more talk, her brother said. She convinced him, though, that Oren's accident had created the necessity; otherwise, it would never have occurred to her to try. And as for the gossipy old ladies in town, well, they should count their blessings. Your whole life could change in the blink of an eye.

Her brother showed her the basics with the engine off. They were parked in Lily's sloping front yard. Even Lily had to admit that her mechanical reasoning didn't inspire a lot of confi-dence. Gearshifts and clutches and steering wheels were all a bit much for her. But her brother made her repeat all the motions with grim determination. It was, after all, his car that she would be borrowing. Driving was the simplest thing in the world, he kept telling her, certainly simpler than running their mother's old treadle sewing machine. Lily held her tongue. She had never been very good at using the Singer, either. After what seemed like hours of pantomime practice, her brother finally allowed her to turn the engine over. Lily's first attempt to disengage the clutch resulted in the car heaving and bucking halfway to the Peacham Farm Road. Her second attempt wasn't much better, nor was her third. Ian's horses shied to the farthest reaches of their corral, watching suspiciously from a tight huddle. Lily thought it best not to remind her brother that the second-eldest Willard had been killed by a rearing horse at the backfire of a Model T.

Giant soap bubble bursting, translucent multicolored membrane evaporating away. Nothing surrounding her now, nothing buffering her from the real world. Time to make contact, time to ask for help. Clive was his name—the brother who had died. Ryan was the one teaching her to drive now. The eldest was Patrick, then Clive. Robert, Paul and Ryan.

Eventually, Ryan's patience paid off. Lily was able, by sunset, to drive the Ford to her mother's house to pick up Faith. Ryan felt satisfied enough with her progress to give her another lesson the following Saturday. Her spirits lifted, in spite of Faith's grim face and white knuckles gripping the edge of the seat. By the end of the month, she would be driving herself to the hospital in Barre to visit Oren. Up till now, she had been imposing on her father and brothers every other afternoon.

Over Faith's favorite meal, beef stew, Lily explained as cheerfully as she could that Granny would be making dinner for her every other night while Mommy visited Daddy at the hospital. Faith took this news without comment. She had given up on begging to come along. Lily had made it clear: hospitals weren't for little girls. Of course, it was more than that. The prognosis for Oren's recovery was, as yet, unclear. She didn't want her daughter's last memory of her father to be that of a breathing corpse. There was already too much that was strange about Faith's childhood, too much that would not make good memories to comfort her later in life. Lily tried not to stare at Faith as she picked at her plate. It worried her that her daughter seemed so moody and listless, more silent with each passing week. Lily took a deep breath. She feared silence more than just about anything.

"Not hungry?" Lily asked.

"No."

"Me either. Shall we give our plates to the cats?"

Faith smiled and nodded.

"How would you like to learn how to play the fiddle? I could teach you on the nights that I'm home."

"Really?"

"We could start right now."

Lily led Faith to the music room, leaving their supper plates on the kitchen table for the tabby to lick clean. She uncased her fiddle and tuned it. She closed her eyes for a moment and tried to remember how Ian had taught her. She could see them in the milk house: herself, sitting on Ian's knee; him placing his hands over hers and guiding her fingers. She instructed Faith to crawl into her lap. "Our first song will be 'For He's a Jolly Good Fellow,'" she whispered. "You can surprise Daddy with it when he gets home. But first I'm going to teach you the names of the strings." Lily forged ahead, explaining that notes corresponded to letters of the alphabet, even though Faith hadn't yet learned how to read. She pushed aside her one niggling worry—that the best she would ever be able to do was teach Faith how to play second fiddle. And so they began.

That night, she lay sleepless in bed. It seemed so big and empty without Oren. She moved to his side and clutched his pillow in her arms. It didn't help. She lit the bedside lamp. Did she dare? Did she still have his permission? She opened the drawer to his table and took out his leather-bound journal. Just a few words, just a few random words so that she might *feel* his presence again.

> *Identical or fraternal? Two separate eggs, or one split in half? I say Siamese. Same egg, cleaved down the middle but not split in two. We did everything, felt everything, shared everything together. Identical twins are accidental. They're just Siamese twins that get fully separated at birth somehow.*

She closed the book. She put it back in the drawer and shut off the light. Odd really: she knew Oren's body so well; she knew how to read his slightest gesture, the subtleties of his many silences. But she had never really known what he *thought*. Yet with this little book, she could get to know his mind in his absence. She would sleep now, knowing this. She would finally sleep.

She had her dream about the burning barn. This time, though, it wasn't a woman staring out the window. It was Oren, his face flickering pink and orange through the frosty panes. But when she called to him to come back to bed, he stared at her as if he didn't recognize her. Instead, he turned and walked, unconscious, out of the room. It was only then that she realized Oren hadn't answered because it was Ian. Ian sleepwalking again. In the dark they both looked the same. You had to see the scars to be sure.

Lily lay there, willing her heartbeat to return to normal while a film of cold sweat evaporated from her upper lip. She hadn't spoken to either Ian or Hallie since the accident. Needless to say, neither had come by the house to offer the customary condolences or cold dishes. She felt a tear leak from the corner of her eye and drip into her ear. Their poor little baby, still-born on those bloody sheets. She lay there crying and waiting for Faith. Lily wanted more than anything to hold her daughter close. But it was hours before dawn. This wasn't her fault. It wasn't her fault. It wasn't. She wondered at how all of their lives could have taken such a terrible, terrible turn—that even basic human kindness could be ignored. It wasn't right.

Lily closed the library early for her first solo voyage to the hospital. One of the old-timers mumbled, "here she goes again" as he shuffled out. "Damn right," she said and slammed the door behind him. It would make her day to get another letter from the Board of Selectmen relieving her of her duties. She settled into her brother's Ford and revved the engine. If Lindbergh could fly across the Atlantic, she could certainly get herself to Barre. She set off down Route 2 at little better than a crawl. It was a gorgeous early-summer afternoon with everything glittering green and gold. She stopped at the roadside to open all the windows. She found it oddly thrilling to be leaving Cabot Fields under her own power. If she wanted to, she could just keep driving—to Brattle-boro or to Boston. Leave the catastrophe of her life in the shimmering golden dust. She wondered about her new taste for freedom—and why it always took catastrophes to liberate you.

Lily hated the hospital and everything about it: the gleaming corridors of white ceramic tile, the enormous ward of soldiered metal beds, the hollow-eyed men staring at her as she passed by. Their howls, their whimpers, their moans, their stench of piss and sickness. She could only bear to sit with Oren for an hour. The hour was exactly the same with each visit. She drew the flimsy curtain that separated his bed from all the others, she sat in that excruciating wooden chair with no cushion, she took his cold, inert hand in her own and warmed it. She told him about her day—laundry, grocery shopping, the book she was reading, the books the old-timers in the library were reading, her late-night dreams—anything she could think of to fill the sixty minutes that stretched before her. And all the while she watched his closed eyelids carefully for a flutter or twitch, any sign that he knew she was there.

This chatter, she knew, was a way of distracting herself from the horror of seeing him in such a state. It had taken surprisingly little time for all the flesh to melt away from his body, leaving behind a framework of miscellaneous bones held together by a taut waxy layer of skin. She was reminded of Ian, just after his return from the war. But what could you expect from a man who now ate only sugar through a rubber tube inserted into his bruised elbow joint, who moved only when he was rolled onto his side or back by an over-busy nurse? Purple eyelids in hollow purple sockets, crusty purple lips. Ironic that his beard and fingernails seemed to grow twice as fast as normal. To Lily he resembled the ancient vampires of literature, unable to bear the burden of broad daylight.

Tonight when her hour was up, Lily kissed Oren on the forehead, wished him a good night and beat a hasty retreat. She couldn't wait to reach the Ford out in the parking lot. Liberation. There she could take large gulps of night air, several of them, before heading back to Cabot Fields. On her way out, she crossed paths with Old Doc Perry. He had come down to Barre on other business, he said, and had decided to look in on their boy.

"How're those driving lessons working out?" he asked, trying to keep things light.

"I'd rather be in the passenger seat," Lily lied, "especially after dark. But I'm managing okay."

"Just as long as you're careful. We don't need the both of you up in here." They stood for a moment, not knowing what else to say to each other. "How did he look to you tonight?" Doc Perry asked.

"Same as yesterday. Same as tomorrow, probably."

He shrugged and ran a hand through his closely cropped white hair. "Who can say? Fact of the matter is, we still don't know much about Oren's condition. I've had people come out of it after more than a year. I've had them slip away after a couple of weeks."

"It's so frustrating," Lily said. "Not being able to do anything for him."

"But you are, honey. Just by letting him know you're here."

"Sometimes I wonder," Lily said, choking back a sob. She was *not* going to begin blubbering, right there in the middle of the hospital corridor. She had shed far too many useless tears already.

"How about I tell you what I think," Doc Perry said. "You can decide whether it's the ravings of a doddering old charlatan."

Lily nodded.

"I believe this is the way Oren's body has decided to deal with the incredible pain of his fall. He's gone and stored his consciousness in some safe part of his brain, a place where he can't feel pain or regret or remorse—or anything else. And I believe this is a lovely comfortable place to be, so comfortable, in fact, that it's more appealing for him to stay right there than come back to us and grapple with the difficult process of healing. I've always had better success with patients who have relations visiting them every day, coaxing them back. The old guys who don't have anybody don't last long. So in my opinion, you've got to keep coming as often as you can and reminding him what a wonderful life is waiting for him here on this side."

Lily nodded again. She needed to think more about it. But she couldn't possibly do that right now. Air. She needed to get out breathing man, a man with his own heart pumping away, a man like any other—except that this man had struggled all his life to b noticed.

"Oren got a letter too, didn't he?" Lily said with certainty.

"What are you talking about?"

"A draft letter. There were two. Of course there were two You just burned his or threw it away or something. You went t war to cut the tie."

"Now you're really talking crazy."

Maybe she had married the wrong twin. Maybe she woul have been better suited to Ian in the end. But Ian hadn't asked her Oren had. And Ian hadn't waited all of his childhood to propose He hadn't come back to Cabot Fields looking for her. He hadn' given up his nomadic existence to be with her. He hadn't designed and built her a house. Ian had only ever tagged along, thirteen minutes behind. She understood then: that Ian could never save Oren's life. He wasn't strong enough to save his own. He woul only ever be his own man if he were separated from Oren, and from her. Well, Oren couldn't help him with that now. Only Lily could. She needed to love him separately, separately and as brother.

"I had a plan," Lily said. She was floating above the two of them having their nice cup of tea. "Oren's business is falling apart at the seams. My brothers are decent enough carpenters, but they're no housewrights. They need a boss, somebody who can tell them what to do. I was going to ask you to take the business back over. At least until Oren came out of it. And if he didn't, well, I would have sold it or given it to you. Either way, it would have gotten the town to ease up on Hallie. Especially if I started going to church with you again. They would all figure everything was forgiven and forgotten. They'd leave you alone."

"I'm out of the carpentry business," Ian said.

of that corridor reeking of piss. "I'd best be getting back to my daughter," she said.

"You be careful, now," Doc Perry said, continuing down the hallway to Oren's ward.

Lily thought about it more on the long drive back to Cabot Fields. All the windows in the car were open wide. Doc Perry had only meant to be helpful. But in the process he had somehow managed to give Lily one more thing to worry about. If it were true that Oren, the real Oren, was in some safe place, if it were true that he needed to be reminded about all the wonderful things there were to live for, she doubted very seriously that he would open his eyes. She remembered her last words to him: that she had married him, not him and his brother. Not only had this been mean-spirited, but it had not been true. She had married a strange sort of man, a man who had never functioned entirely on his own, a man who had stored his love and spirit, strength and humor in two places. She knew that Oren would not come back for her alone. He would need all of himself—Ian—to pull him back.

These thoughts were fresh in Lily's mind when she saw Hallie crossing the town common the next day. Lily was eating her sandwich, as usual, in the shade of her favorite maple. She watched some of the women from church disband quickly as Hallie approached them. Not entirely sure what she was doing, Lily stood and hailed Hallie. Hallie hesitated, then strode over. She was normally fastidious about her appearance. But her dress was rumpled and more than a few wisps of hair had escaped from her bun.

"I need a word with you," Lily said, when Hallie was nearly upon her.

"What do you want?"

"I just want you to know that I don't bear you any ill will." Hallie laughed harshly. Lily nonetheless bolstered her courage and carried on. "What's happened to us—to all of us—it's terrible. I think we should just pull together as a family now."

Hallie placed her hands on her hips. She stared at Lily with too-bright eyes, eyes that seemed to flash from side to side though they were not moving. "And just how are we going to do that?" Hallie said. "Now that you've turned most of the town against me?"

"I haven't, Hallie. I haven't spoken a bad word."

"Is that so? Then how do you explain the fact that I can't get anyone to give me the time of day around here? Why is it that when I want to buy flour in the store they seem to have just run out—or when Ian needs grain for the horses, they're not extending any more credit until after the harvest? How do you reckon that in the past month, five of our steady customers have all decided not to stable with us anymore?"

"You've done all that yourself."

Hallie stared at her in wonder. "You really believe that, don't you?" she said. "Somehow, you still manage to think that it's everyone else's fault. Poor misunderstood Lily. As if you haven't been right at the center of this little drama, pulling the puppet strings the entire time."

"That's so unkind."

"Get out of my way, Lily."

"Hallie, I can help you. I can make them stop. And you can help me—or at least Ian can. He can bring Oren around again, just by visiting him once in a while and talking to him. That's what Old Doc Perry says."

"Why on earth would I want Oren to get better?" Hallie said. "Things suit me just fine the way they are. I say, a life for a life. I say, welcome to my misery, sister." With that, Hallie stepped around Lily and continued across the common without looking back.

—

But Lily's plan worked. Because a few days later Ian stopped by the library, just before closing. No one else was there; the old-timers had gotten used to being kicked out early. Lily invited him into the back room for a cup of tea.

"How's my brother doing?" he asked, staring into his mug.

"He needs you," she said. She explained what Doc Perry had told her, what she wanted him to do.

"Sounds like a lot of horseshit to me," he said. But she could tell by the look on his face that he had stored it away to mull over later, in private. Oren had always done the same.

"I'm not asking you to believe any of it. I'm just asking you to try."

Ian paused. He looked up from his tea and met Lily's eyes, just like Hallie had done on the common. But there was a little kindness there, and a whole lot more pain. "I'm not always crazy about the results when you rope me into things," he said.

"He's your brother," Lily whispered.

"He got everything," Ian said. "I always got what was left over."

Silence so heavy that Lily could hear her own heart.

"He didn't get everything."

"He got you."

She flushed. She experienced a rush of memories—little moments—of wiping his forehead while they were haying, of combing down lame old Dan together side-by-side, of anticipating a mistletoe kiss at their one and only Christmas party—and she wasn't prepared for it. She had never thought to look at things from Ian's point of view. Until this very moment, she had seen his personality as an extension of Oren's. She had loved him for his music and his dry wit, his fearlessness, his sensuality. But she had never considered these traits to belong to him alone. In her mind, she had always given them over to Oren. Suddenly she saw Ian for the man he was, maybe for the first time, surely too late: a living,

"Yes. I see that now," Lily said, "Why did you come here today?"

"I know you didn't kill my baby. I know you wouldn't do that."

"No," Lily whispered. "I would never do that."

"I'll be going now. Hallie gets worried." He stood to leave.

Ian might have wanted her once. He might have also believed that she was better suited to him than his brother. But now he loved Hallie—that was clear. For him, Hallie had not merely been a convenient way to get the town off their backs. She had become someone for him and him alone. Another attempt at cutting the tie. Neither Lily nor Oren had understood that. Why hadn't they seen that?

"Ian," she said, wiping a tear away with her sleeve. "There's something else. Faith is crazy about horses. She stops by your corral every morning—"

"She feeds them sugar. I watch the two of you from the barn. She's a beautiful little girl. She looks just like me."

Lily surprised herself by laughing. He joined in. Of course Faith looked like him.

"Will you teach her to ride, Ian? I don't want her to grow up not knowing how."

"Lily, I'm not going to visit Oren. And it's not because Hallie has forbidden it—"

"I know. I'm not talking about that. I'm talking about riding lessons. And then maybe a few fiddling lessons, when I can't take her any farther."

"I'll have to ask Hallie what she thinks."

"I know."

Lily watched him go. She had married the right man. She could bear everything else, now. Even if Oren died, even if she spent the rest of her life alone. Because in the end, everyone died alone.

—

Lily resigned from the library the very next day. She wrote out a letter and left it propped against the brass lamp on her desk. Then she had her two younger brothers, Paul and Ryan, over to The Knoll. She made them supper, while her mother looked after Faith. She informed them she would be taking over the daily operations of Pritchard Brothers. They raised all the expected objections—that she didn't know a thing about carpentry or running a business—and she shot back her prepared response: neither did they. But she was a woman, they argued. She told them she was well aware of that fact. They threatened to take the matter to their father. She fired them both on the spot. They backed down a little, then. They told her to be reasonable; with a little time, they could get things back in order themselves. She informed them they had two choices: work with her, or start looking for other work. They told her she would regret it, but they stayed for dessert. Over cobbler, she grilled them about each of their current projects and who in town owed them money. She insisted they only turn up for work at the paying jobs. She gave them coffee, and then she sent them home.

She felt lighter, somehow, on the walk to her parents' house to collect Faith. Her mother was in the kitchen, doing the supper dishes. She asked Lily how things were. Lily said, better; things were a little better. Her mother told her that Faith was up playing in her old room. Lily took the stairs.

She listened at the doorway to Faith's tea party. They must all be good, she told Lily's ancient dolls, or their father wouldn't wake up from a spell that had been placed on him. Lily flushed with rage. She would have a word with her mother later. As if any of this were Faith's fault! To calm herself, Lily began tracing the scrollwork of the door frame with her fingertips. She had never really noticed how intricate the woodwork was, though she had passed through this threshold thousands of times. Fanciful stalks fluted upward, sprouting tiny leaves along the way, blossoming out in a bouquet of unlikely lilies.

She reached for Oren's journal in the drawer, then stopped herself. She had been reading a little of it every night. She had learned what he thought about so many things: neoclassical architecture, small-town life, the industrial revolution, child-rearing. She only allowed herself a page or two, a single entry to get herself through another day. But it wasn't the same at all—his mind—not the same as his big warm body, his long arms around her, his morning hardness resting on her buttocks. Her fingers wandered to her belly. They hiked up her nightgown and wandered lower. She closed her eyes and sighed. This wasn't the same either. It still felt like waiting. But if she had to wait for Oren, she would not allow herself to grow helpless and pathetic. She would take care of herself, damnit. Think for herself.

She sent out invoices for all the overdue work. She paid calls to those customers who didn't send by post what they owed Pritchard Brothers. Soon enough her neighbors realized they would be dealing with her if they wanted a mother-in-law room added to the back of their house, or an indoor toilet. Some went elsewhere for their carpentry. Most couldn't be bothered. It was widely agreed that Lily cut a fair price for a woman. And Pritchard Brothers did the best work.

She bought a radio. She wanted to know what was going on in the world. She put it in the kitchen and listened to the news every night while she did the supper dishes. Amelia Earhart became the first woman to fly across the Atlantic. A recent study showed that thirty-four out of thirty-five lung cancer patients were also heavy smokers. The first all-talking film, *The Lights of New York*, was previewed in Manhattan. Another influenza epidemic was killing thousands. It comforted her, somehow, that every single day offered up as many triumphs as tragedies.

Late one August afternoon, she found herself pacing impatiently on the front porch. She was late for her visit with Oren. Everything had already gone a dusty salmon: the sky, the dirt of the drive, the windshield of the Ford, the hayfields bordering either side. Soon her father would be bringing his new Farmall tractor across the road—the first in the area—for the last mowing. Still no sign of Faith and Ian. Where were they?

Lily had begun sending Faith down to Ian's stables after lunch. Faith helped out in the barn for a couple of hours, soaping saddles and laying fresh hay. After that, they usually went on a ride together. Sometimes Hallie packed them a little snack. When they got home, Lily would have a cup of tea with Faith, usually out on the front porch, and then send her off to her mother's for supper before driving to the hospital.

Lily seated herself on the porch swing. She tried to put images of Faith being pitched over paddock fences out of her mind. Ian only let her ride Old Dan, who was now so lame he couldn't break into a trot if he wanted to. She jammed her hands into the pockets of her apron to keep from gnawing at her poor nails. The soapstone. She felt it clank against her engagement ring—Oren's mother's ring. She experienced an odd moment of vertigo, then. She closed her eyes to stave off the dizziness. Spiraling, spiraling into the center of something she didn't understand, something the size of a silver dollar, stopping only at a hole bored into its center, stopping finally at nothing.

You see more than you let on. Lily knew suddenly and with certainty that Mme. LeTourneau had just died. And she knew she would not tell anyone about it when the news spread around town.

She heard a shout and opened her eyes. There they were! Faith was in the lead, waving her arm. Lily bolted up from the swing. She began walking toward them, ready to scold. All thoughts of this, however, fled from her mind when she saw what Faith was holding: a tarnished tin bell. The two of them had ridden to the abandoned cemetery that afternoon. Ian had told her the story about the Indians and the original settlers. They had lain quietly in the leaves and loam, listening for bells. Faith had found one.

Lily helped her daughter to dismount. Faith asked if she could stay a little longer and help muck out the stall. Lily said no. Another time, maybe. Tonight they were in a hurry. She reminded Faith to thank her uncle Ian. Ian, the very picture of health: a gigantic man with broad shoulders and muscular arms. Golden hair flopping over a strong brow, long thin nose, chiseled jaw; almond-shaped eyes fringed in long lashes, like a girl's. Another time, maybe. But not now. Now, Lily needed to get to Barre. She needed to sit with her husband. Oren needed to know she was there—there for him.

Ian told Faith he would see her tomorrow. Lily took Faith's hand. Together they began the long walk up the hill. Lily could feel Ian's eyes the entire way. She didn't look back. She just kept walking.

In the front yard, Faith stopped and turned to Lily. She asked if it was true, that her daddy had proposed to her in that gloomy old cemetery. Lily nodded. When had Oren finally told Ian that part of the story? Twins.

"I miss Daddy," Faith said. "When is he coming home?"

Lily knelt. She wanted to face her daughter, eye-to-eye. "You're a big girl now, aren't you?" she said. Faith nodded. "I have another surprise for you. Something special—just like the bell you found." She fished the soapstone from her apron pocket and pressed it into her daughter's hand.

"What is it?" Faith asked.

"It's you and me," Lily said. "A secret, just between the two of us." She told Faith to run into the house; she would need to wash her face and hands before they got going. Faith was old enough now to start visiting her father in the hospital—a big girl. Faith dashed up the porch steps and into the house. Lily followed slowly, refusing to worry about whether she was doing the right thing.

It was a long drive, and during it, Lily tried to prepare Faith for what lay ahead. Daddy probably wouldn't look like the person she remembered, she said. He was very sick. Faith asked her when he was going to get better. Lily thought for a moment before answering. He might not, she said. No one knows for sure. Faith stared out the passenger window, thinking that over. Well, I think he should get better, she said. Lily could not answer. The words would not come. All the things she had said. All the things she had not said. Especially that one thing, the thing he might need to hear the most.

"I love your daddy very much," Lily whispered. "You know that, don't you?"

Faith nodded. They rode the rest of the way in silence.

The two of them held hands as they made their way down the long corridors to Oren's ward. Faith was silent, but she didn't seem afraid until they passed all the old men, grinning at her and chuckling. Lily squeezed her daughter's hand for reassurance. Faith squeezed it back. She whirled on the nearest old man. Stop staring! she shouted. Silence descended on the ward. Come on, Mommy, she said. Lily let her daughter lead the way forward, wishing she had thought of this months ago.

Faith took the wooden chair next to Oren; Lily perched at the windowsill. Faith sat quietly for a moment, staring at his face, holding his hand. But soon she began to kick her legs out of boredom. Lily looked at her watch, doubting that they would make it through the entire hour.

"But this is never going to wake him up," Faith said, suddenly.

"Shh, we won't stay much longer," Lily whispered back.

"Don't whisper," Faith said. "He won't be able to hear you." She stood up. "Wake up, Daddy," she said, shaking his hand.

"Faith!"

"Wake up!"

"Faith, stop that! You'll disturb all the other nice people around us."

Faith ignored her. Instead, she pulled the tin bell out of the front pocket of her dress and began ringing it next to Oren's ear. "Wake up, I said. It's time to wake up, Daddy!"

Lily knew that she should snatch the bell away from her daughter. She should spank her for being so naughty. But she was speechless.

Because Oren's eyelids had begun to flutter.

And in this flutter she sees a flicker of light. And an old dream comes back to her, of the rosy fluttering and flickering of flames on glass. And she is once again staring out a window. Only this time it isn't her bedroom window—she can see that now—it is the windshield of a dilapidated caravan. And the roof that is on fire doesn't belong to Ian's horse barn. It is the roof of her own house. It is the house she lives in now, but it is also the little house she was born in, the one where she lived most of her childhood before her father built a new one. She watches herself setting fire to these houses with a torch Oren has handed her. Now the three of them are sitting in the cab of the caravan, smiling, watching everything burn to the ground. Ready? Ian asks. Oren and Lily nod. Ian throws the truck into gear and drives out of the yard. He takes a left onto the Peacham Farm Road. They are headed for parts unknown, all the hammers and saws, ladders and lanterns, pots and pans clattering merrily behind them. They disappear into the smoke.

Lily lets go. She lets the dream evaporate—tears drying at the corners of her eyes. She can dream it again and again for as long as she lives, in the privacy of the bathtub or her vegetable garden. But she must stay here now, in this moment. She cannot concern herself with the next until it comes. Because her husband's eyelids are fluttering. His eyes are about to open.

In every corner of the world, on every subject under the sun, Penguin represents quality and variety—the very best in publishing today.

For complete information about books available from Penguin—including Puffins, Penguin Classics, and Compass—and how to order them, write to us at the appropriate address below. Please note that for copyright reasons the selection of books varies from country to country.

In the United Kingdom: Please write to *Dept. EP, Penguin Books Ltd, Bath Road, Harmondsworth, West Drayton, Middlesex UB7 0DA.*

In the United States: Please write to *Penguin Putnam Inc., P.O. Box 12289 Dept. B, Newark, New Jersey 07101-5289* or call 1-800-788-6262.

In Canada: Please write to *Penguin Books Canada Ltd, 10 Alcorn Avenue, Suite 300, Toronto, Ontario M4V 3B2.*

In Australia: Please write to *Penguin Books Australia Ltd, P.O. Box 257, Ringwood, Victoria 3134.*

In New Zealand: Please write to *Penguin Books (NZ) Ltd, Private Bag 102902, North Shore Mail Centre, Auckland 10.*

In India: Please write to *Penguin Books India Pvt Ltd, 11 Panchsheel Shopping Centre, Panchsheel Park, New Delhi 110 017.*

In the Netherlands: Please write to *Penguin Books Netherlands bv, Postbus 3507, NL-1001 AH Amsterdam.*

In Germany: Please write to *Penguin Books Deutschland GmbH, Metzlerstrasse 26, 60594 Frankfurt am Main.*

In Spain: Please write to *Penguin Books S. A., Bravo Murillo 19, 1° B, 28015 Madrid.*

In Italy: Please write to *Penguin Italia s.r.l., Via Benedetto Croce 2, 20094 Corsico, Milano.*

In France: Please write to *Penguin France, Le Carré Wilson, 62 rue Benjamin Baillaud, 31500 Toulouse.*

In Japan: Please write to *Penguin Books Japan Ltd, Kaneko Building, 2-3-25 Koraku, Bunkyo-Ku, Tokyo 112.*

In South Africa: Please write to *Penguin Books South Africa (Pty) Ltd, Private Bag X14, Parkview, 2122 Johannesburg.*